WORLD IN TORMENT

Atomic war! It had been instituted by men — overriding the desires of women and plunging the world into destruction. Finally — the vast armies shattered, women succeed as rulers, and under successive Matriarchs the world recovers. To maintain global peace the Matriarch employs official assassins under the chief of Security Police. But when orders are issued for the assassination of the apparently harmless Don Burgarde, her personal secretary Lyra decides to intervene . . . The seeds of rebellion are being sown . . .

Books by E. C. Tubb
in the Linford Mystery Library:

ASSIGNMENT NEW YORK
THE POSSESSED
THE LIFE BUYER
DEAD WEIGHT
DEATH IS A DREAM
MOON BASE
FEAR OF STRANGERS
TIDE OF DEATH
FOOTSTEPS OF ANGELS
THE SPACE-BORN
SECRET OF THE TOWERS
THE PRICE OF FREEDOM

E. C. TUBB

WORLD IN TORMENT

Complete and Unabridged

LINFORD
Leicester

First published in Great Britain

First Linford Edition
published 2008

British Library CIP Data

Tubb, E. C.
　　World in torment.—Large print ed.—
　　Linford mystery library
　　1. Assassination—Fiction 2. Matriachy—
　　Fiction 3. Dissenters—Fiction 4. Dystopias
　　5. Large type books
　　I. Title
　　823.9'14 [F]

ISBN 978–1–84782–449–3

Published by
F. A. Thorpe (Publishing)
Anstey, Leicestershire

Set by Words & Graphics Ltd.
Anstey, Leicestershire
Printed and bound in Great Britain by
T. J. International Ltd., Padstow, Cornwall

This book is printed on acid-free paper

1

Lyra

The room was warm, softly lit, and seemed to be vibrant with hidden life. From a concealed speaker a low voice murmured a continuous stream of news items, the emotionless tones whispering through the thick silence.

'Food production from eastern sea farms shows continuous decrease of ten percent per harvest. Green riots in Central Europe at proposed building of volcanic power pits. Election results from South America shows feminist element on the ascendancy. Astronomers predict unequalled sun spot activity will result in severe ionic storms . . . '

Behind a wide desk ringed with instruments and covered with papers, a woman sat in deep concentration. A tall, slender woman, no longer young but as yet unmarred by age. Thick black hair fell

1

in soft ripples to narrow shoulders. Her skin had a faint bronze cast, and her oddly slanted eyes were as black as ebony.

She wore a uniform of slacks and high collared blouse, belted at the waist, and all of deep black. A faint pattern of thin gold lines weaved in an intricate arabesque over the entire uniform, relieving the sombre colouring. A wide band of gold was clasped to her left wrist, supporting an elaborate chronometer, her long thin fingers were devoid of rings, and her nails lacked varnish.

She would have been beautiful in any age, but in one where females aped the male, she was more than just beautiful. She knew it, knew also the antagonism it aroused, but deliberately ignored it. It was one of the advantages of her position that she was able to do so.

Papers rustled as she scanned them, seeming only to glance at the columns of figures, but actually remembering every slightest detail. The low murmuring voice from the concealed speaker registered itself without conscious effort, and even as she both saw and heard, a portion of her mind was busy with her own private thoughts.

A light flashed on one of the instruments before her, even as it died she threw the switch on the intercom.

'Yes?'

'Lyra, come in here.'

'At once.'

She opened the circuit, rose from the chair, and with a supple easy grace moved across the room. A door swung open before her, harsh light streaming full into her face, narrowing her eyes a little against the glare. Three steps more and she stared down at the Matriarch of the Western Federation.

The door hissed shut behind her.

Mary Beamish, Third Matriarch of the Western Federation, was an old woman, and looked it. Her sparse grey hair was cropped, parted and dressed as a man's. She wore an unflattering uniform of thick rough tweeds, a shirt, collar and tie, with heavy shoes. Her lined features sagged and her little pale eyes were surrounded with a maze of tiny lines. Her figure was broad and shapeless. She had a plain wristwatch strapped to one thick wrist, and the nails of her hands were bitten almost to the quick. Against her, Lyra was a vision of perfection, a woman against something that was neither man nor woman.

Instinctively the Matriarch bridled.

'I haven't seen you before have I?' Her voice was harsh and thin, like that of a very old man, or a very young boy. Lyra smiled.

'No, Madam. You were elected only yesterday, and as yet have had little time to take up your duties.' Deliberately she sat down.

'You were here during the time of my predecessor, weren't you?'

'Yes, Madam.'

'I've heard about you, supposed to be very efficient aren't you.' It was more of a statement than a question.

'I have been found so.'

'Don't give yourself airs my girl!' The old woman glared her dislike. 'I can replace you, there are a dozen women who could do your work, women who wouldn't dress as you do.' The sagging

4

features pursed as if from a nasty taste. 'Do you have to dress like that?'

'My clothes hardly determine my efficiency,' Lyra said mildly. 'I have had the honour to serve the duly elected Matriarchs for a long time now. If for no other reason than that I am able to act as your informant, it would not be easy to replace me without causing some disruption.' She smiled and leaned forward a little.

'Your period of office is only for three years. Would it be wise to waste valuable time? After all results are what count at election time, and your majority was not a large one.'

'You're right.' The old woman nodded her head. 'That Jones woman would like to indict me for inefficiency, she has a dangerously large following in the feminist movement.' She frowned. 'Something should be done about that woman.'

'As Matriarch, something could be.' The suggestion in Lyra's voice was unmistakable.

'The assassins you mean?'

'Call them your Security Police.'

'Call them what you like, but they still kill people don't they?'

'Sometimes,' admitted Lyra. 'Sometimes it is the only wav to prevent war.'

'War!' Anger suffused the Matriarch's heavy features. 'War is a thing born of men. We women want none of it. To see our children torn from our arms, fed to the ravening cannon, to die on foreign fields far from their loved ones. To see overgrown children strut and clown in uniforms, playing with the lives of those yet unborn!' She paused, breathing heavily. 'Don't ever mention war to me again.'

'And yet war there will be unless precautions are taken.'

'There must be no war!'

With surprising agility for one so gross, the old woman swung from her chair, and gestured at the high window.

'Look! There, low on the horizon. See it? See that blue glow? A city once stood there, a city of over eight million people. Come now. All gone. Dissolved in the blue flame of radioactive destruction, and it was not the only one. All over the world

6

great pits stream forth their deadly radiation, square miles where no living thing dare tread. And that isn't all. What of the sterile soil? The vast tracts where radioactive dusts were spread, what of them?'

'We are reclaiming that soil,' said Lyra gently.

'But so slowly. Can we wait that long? Dare we wait while famine snarls at our heels?'

'What else can we do but wait?'

'There are things I could suggest.' Weakly the old woman slumped back into her chair. 'One of the first must be the complete elimination of all none-producers. Food is too scarce to allow the crippled, the insane, the freaks to live. We will cut the ration, less for men than for women. It will be hard, but it is the only way.'

'Is that fair?' Lyra protested. 'The atom war took place during the last generation, over forty years ago, how can you blame those alive now?'

'Men started the war. Men overrode the desires of their women and plunged the world into an orgy of destruction. It could have been the end of civilisation, almost it was, but for a miracle it would have been.'

'Lucy Westcott?'

'Yes.' The Matriarch almost whispered the name, a sudden gentleness softening her harsh features. 'Lucy Westcott. A heroine, a martyr. It was she who aroused the women to revolt. When the vast armies of men had finally been shattered by atomic bombardment, it was she who demanded that women be allowed to rule. The vote gave her power, as First Matriarch she negotiated an armistice, turned all the vast war potential into peaceful production. Her assassination was the most criminal thing that men ever did.'

'It was never proved that a man fired the shot which killed her.'

'What woman could have done so? There wasn't a woman on the Earth who wouldn't have gladly died for her. No. Men killed her, and men must pay for that crime.'

In the sudden silence the muted

murmur of a strato-plane echoed softly through the air. Lights blazed from the landing field, and the whistling roar of wide open jets penetrated even the soundproofed walls. Lyra stirred uneasily, her thoughts busy as she correlated several new aspects into a new pattern of conduct.

Mary Beamish was a fanatic. That in itself wasn't unusual, most women who sublimated every natural urge to the fulfilment of ambition usually were, but the new Matriarch was more than that. Coupled with ambition was hate. Hate of men. It was a blind unreasoning hatred, and unfortunately one shared by too many women. In the natural desire to place the blame for the world's condition on a scapegoat, men had been chosen. It was a dangerous thing, dangerous because it cut across all natural instincts.

Men could be hated, but they were still men, and because of that simple fact, still essential. To hate what you wanted to love, and love what you thought you should hate, led to mental conflict, a conflict so intense as to be impossible of compromise. To continue that conflict must lead to but one thing.

Insanity.

Individually that wouldn't have been too bad, but Mary Beamish was not alone in her dislike of men. It was the basis of the Feminist movement, and almost all of the female world population had joined it. A growing wave of anti-male hysteria was sweeping the world. Men were regarded as fools, idiots, criminals. To marry was to invite scorn, to divorce approbation. Legal laws were framed to safeguard women, and women only. Children were taking their mother's name, from the Matriarch down, women had taken control, and the trend was growing fast.

The old woman was speaking and Lyra adjusted her thoughts.

'As my secretary and advisor what needs to be done now?'

'There are several documents needing your signature.' Lyra gestured towards a sheaf of papers on the wide desk. 'The allocations of labour to the sea farms. Approval to the volcanic power project.

General amnesty for all declared mutants.'

'Wait!' The old woman studied the papers before her. 'Sea farm labour. I see that you have mentioned a labour increase of twenty percent. Why?'

'Production is falling at a ten percent per harvest figure. As you know, men are the best workers for the sea farms, they are able to withstand the pressure of the deep water levels better than women. Twenty percent added labour should stabilise the production level.'

'I see.' The pen made heavy scratching sounds as the old woman scrawled her signature at the foot of the document. 'Where are you going to get the extra labour?'

'The recruitment officers will take care of that.' Lyra removed the signed papers and proffered others. 'The approbation for the volcanic power project.'

'It seems rather high,' protested the old woman, 'do they need all this?'

'Yes. With the exhaustion of coal and oil we are getting desperate for power. Atomics need refined ores, and atomic piles are not popular. Volcanic power

11

offers us all the safe cheap power we need.'

'It still seems a tremendous amount.'

'The initial cost is high,' admitted Lyra, 'but the results will be worth it. Remember that we are having to drill pits into the surface three miles deep. Then water must be piped to the pits, generating plant installed, and a network of power cables built to enmesh the entire world.'

'What progress has been made so far?'

'The cables have been built, that was the simplest part of the plan. Several pits have been dug, and three at least are working. As you know water is piped into them, generating hydroelectric power as it falls. The temperature at the bottom of the pits is high enough to convert the water into steam, and so the steam not only blasts itself from the pit, but can be used to operate turbines as it does so. Ultimately we hope to have a self-contained system. Water falling into the pits, being converted into steam, circulating through the turbines, condensing back into water, and falling into the pit again.'

'I see.' Again the pen scratehed. 'What else?'

'This amnesty for all mutants.'

'No.'

'Why not?'

'They are non-producers.'

'They cannot help what they are, they did not ask to be born. There are hundreds of them, ostracised, hounded, many are living in the dead lands. It would be common charity to recognise them for what they are, and offer them sanctuary.'

'They are monsters.'

'They are our own children,' corrected Lyra. 'Their parents were human, their chromosomes distorted by the free radiations of the atom war. It is not the fault of the mutants that they are what they are.'

'What do you suggest we do with them?'

'Offer them freedom. Give them a tract of land to live out their own destiny. Most of them are sterile, they will die without children. Others are doomed to an early death, their bodies too far from normal to survive for long, A few are geniuses, those few we can use, but to get them we must show some degree of humanity.'

'And if they turn on us, destroy us as some seem to think they may, what then?'

'Then we deserve to be destroyed. Either we are strong enough to withstand such an attack, or our civilisation is too weak to be worth saving anyway.' Abruptly Lyra laughed, her tones high and clear. 'Are we children to be afraid of shadows?'

'I'll decide later,' grunted the old woman thrusting aside the papers. 'Now I have a plan of my own.'

'Yes?'

'I have been compiling a list of names of those who are dangerous to the peace and safety of the world. I want them eliminated.'

'Assassinated?'

'Must you call it that?' The Matriarch frowned. 'It sounds nasty, and I hate nasty things. I just want them put out of the way.'

'I understand,' Lyra held out her

slender hand. 'Give me the list, I'll take care of them for you.'

Briefly she studied the long list of names, then glanced sharply at the squat figure of the old woman.

'All of these?'

'Yes.'

Slowly Lyra returned the paper, the old woman watching her from her pale little eyes.

'What's the matter?'

'I suggest that you get rid of personal desires for vengeance,' the secretary said grimly. 'You have the names of some of the foremost statesmen alive on that list.'

'What of it? They are men aren't they?'

'Meaning that they are useless anyway?' Slowly Lyra shook her head. 'I know that it is a temptation to avenge ourselves on imagined insult, but it is the wrong thing to do. As Matriarch you should be above such human frailty. What does it matter to you that a woman named Jones once slighted you? Haven't you proved that you are better than she is? Does it matter that Doctor Moray is a man? He is also in sole charge of the volcanic power project, will you endanger that for the mere accident that he is a man?'

'It isn't because of that,' snapped the old woman

'He is working for you, isn't that enough?'

'I am Matriarch,' snapped the old woman. 'Do as I order.'

'Very well. I'll see that the assassins have their orders. Is there anything more?'

'No.'

'Then I may leave now?'

'Get out!'

'As you wish. Goodnight, Madam.'

The old woman didn't answer, but glared from her little eyes at the regal figure of her secretary. Shame, mingled with spiteful hate struggled on the heavy features. Arrogance, coupled with jealousy and a pathetic envy mirrored themselves on her plain face.

'Wait!'

'Yes, Madam?'

'Forget the list. Forget it I say.'

'Yes, Madam. Anything else?'

'Get out of here!'

'Goodnight, Madam.'

Softly the door closed between them.

2

The Killer

It was good to be alone, to be back in the snug warmth of her own room. The light was restful after the harsh glare favoured by the Matriarch, and it was good not to feel the jarring impact of a mind not quite sane. The low murmur still whispered from the concealed speaker, and for a moment she concentrated on what it said.

'Professor Whitehead died from heart failure at his home today. His death will necessitate a new election and it is certain that the feminist group will win. Three men committed suicide after being divorced. Labour unrest at the sterile soil sites has been blamed on Green influence. A new law makes inheritance descend through the female side of the family, hereditary titles will descend to the eldest daughter instead of the eldest son. The death penalty has been decreed for all crimes against women . . . '

Lyra sighed, and switched off the speaker. Silence seemed to fill the room with an almost material solidity. For a moment she rested at the wide desk, supporting her head within the cradle of her hands, then abruptly stirring, Lyra pressed concealed buttons beneath the rim of the desk.

A panel opened a crack, she slid it back and removed two tiny instruments. One she clipped behind her ear, where it rested hidden by the thick black hair. The other she pressed to her throat.

Power surged for a moment, then . . .

'Yes?' The voice echoed emotionlessly against the bone behind her ear, sounding like the faint buzz of a tiny insect.

'Contact three eight seven.' Her voice died even as it reached her lips.

'Contact three eight seven. Proceed.'

'Report. As suspected, unstable mentality, strong traces of paranoia, emotional, potentially dangerous.'

'Nothing unsuspected,' whispered the voice. 'Assumption of power can however render any prognosis useless.'

'Revenge fixation?'

'Strong. Immediate list of more than twenty names. List recalled and there is no immediate danger.'

'Should we guard?'

'Some. Others of no importance. Names to guard as follows: Doctor Moray. Sam Weston. D'Bracy. Fenniss.'

'Are you accepted?'

'For the moment. Suggest usual procedure in such cases.'

'It will be attended to. Report finished?'

'Finished. Off.'

The power died. The tiny voice died, and for a moment Lyra felt terribly alone. Shrugging, she replaced the instruments, closed the panel, and straightened as a soft knock sounded from the outer door.

'Enter.'

The door swung wide and a man strode into the room.

'Are you free?'

'Certainly.' Lyra smiled at him and gestured towards a chair. He grunted slightly as he settled into the cushioned softness, for a moment they stared at each other in unashamed interest.

19

Like all men he was attracted by her beauty, by the soft ripples of her hair, the faint bronze of her skin and the enigmatic pools of her eyes. Yet he did not look at her as a man looks at a woman, his was the gaze of a connoisseur of beauty, the frank stare of the art lover rather than the calculating gaze of the potential lover. He admired her and yet he respected her more.

In turn she stared at him. He was noticeable only by his utter lack of character, his extreme ordinariness. If ever there had been a Mr. Average, this was him. A man of medium height, of medium colouring, of medium weight Thin brown hair swept back from a round face almost pudgy in its smooth rotundity. Eyes of neutral hue stared from either side of a nose without any definite shape. To describe him would be to describe a thousand men, and yet no description could do him justice.

He was the chief of the Security Police, the head of the official assassins, a man who had killed more often than any other man in history. A man who had carried murder to a fine art.

'Have you seen her yet?' He gestured towards the closed inner door.

'Yes. Have you?'

'Just left.' His voice was calm, rather deep, and wholly pleasant, the voice of a man who never permitted himself to feel emotion.

'What do you think?'

He shrugged. 'Much the same as them all. She will keep me busy, and my last job will probably be to eliminate myself.' He shivered a little. 'I don't like it, Lyra. The woman's not quite sane.'

'Why do you say that, Le Roy?'

'Her fanatical hatred of men.' He smiled a little at her expression. 'Don't misunderstand me, I just work here, the people elect their own rulers, and they get the rulers they deserve, but sometimes I wonder if they know just what they are getting.'

'You should know all about that,' she said quietly.

He smiled. 'I plead guilty to being what I am, and yet am I so bad? What would you rather have, screaming politicians urging their peoples on to destructive war, or a quiet funeral for one? We cannot afford armies now, Lyra. We certainly cannot afford another war. If a little subtle assassination can keep the earth free of war and destruction, who can say that it is wrong?'

'I do not sneer at your profession,' she said quickly. 'You know that. Perhaps because I am a woman, and care nothing for honour or martial glory. If a man wants to fight, then let him fight, but let him fight on his own. If the death of one person can ease the lives of many, then it is right that that person should die, but . . . ?'

'A system is only as good as those who practise it.' He smiled, and nodded at her expression. 'I know what you are going to say. There is too much abuse of the Security Police, too many Matriarchs have used the assassins for their own personal feuds. I know it, and yet what can I do?'

'Perhaps nothing, perhaps much.' She mused, staring at the night shrouded windows. 'Other rulers have been destroyed by their own creations. A sword is a two edged blade, and those who live by it . . . '

'Can die by it.' Le Roy finished grimly. 'Don't worry, I'll not assassinate the Matriarch, you can't kill an office, only a person, and the devil you know is better than the one you don't.' He smiled again, 'In any case I think that you can keep our new ruler from excess.' For a while they smiled at each other, both understanding perfectly the unspoken words between them.

'Why do you kill?' Lyra asked abruptly.

'Why do you eat?' He countered. 'I don't know why, I only know that I do. In other ages, other times, I would have been either a soldier of fortune, or a criminal, perhaps even a hero. I can't explain it. I only know that I kill painlessly, mercilessly, and efficiently. Call it pride, call it egotism, call it insanity, call it what you will. I am a killer, and fortunately for me, an official one.'

'How did you feel when first you killed?'

'Feel?' He laughed curtly. 'I didn't feel.'

He slumped deeper in the chair, his eyes muddy pits of remembrance. 'It was my father. A long time ago. We lived on the edge of the dead lands, and we used to forage for food among the ruins. One day he must have gone too far, perhaps his geiger had broken, perhaps he was just desperate for something to feed me with, I was very young at the time, whatever it was he went too far, stayed too long. He was dying when he came out.'

Silence fell, the thick heavy silence of traversed years. 'You have seen the effects of radiant poisoning, you know what it does to the skin, the bones, the eyes, you know how he must have looked, what he must have felt. I stood it for as long as I could, hearing his screams, his pleading for an easy death. I was a dutiful son, and I loved my father. It was so simple to do as he asked. When it was over I felt a terrible relief. It was as if I had done exactly the right thing, as if I was blessed.' He paused, his voice thick and unsteady. 'I have never regretted my action.'

'And then you killed again, and again?'

'For food, then for warmth, then

because I had to. Finally because I am paid to kill, and because I like to kill.' The round features grew tense with hidden strain.

'Let them all die. Let the earth recapture some of its lost glories. What is man? What has he done with his heritage? Filth scrabbling among filth. Animals, worse than any animal. Insane creatures of hate and lust and blind, wanton stupidity! I hate mankind! I'd like to wipe the slate clean, let the animals have a chance, the birds, the insects. They at least make no pretence of justifying their stupid cruelty.'

'I see.' Lyra stared at the figure before her, and felt the jarring impact of disturbed mentalities on the delicate structure of her brain. Le Roy was mad, The Matriarch was mad. Sometimes she thought the whole world was mad, and that she would go mad with them. She forced herself to smile.

'What are you going to do now?'

'What?' Le Roy blinked, then sat upright in his chair. He had already forgotten what he had spoken about. 'She

25

gave me an assignment, some man she wants eliminated, a routine job.'

'Do I know him?'

'Can't see how you can. He's a nonentity, a local pilot five hundred miles from here. It shouldn't take long.'

'His name?'

'Burgarde. Don Burgarde. Twenty-eight years of age, unmarried, harmless. Heaven knows why she wants him killed, perhaps he forgot to smile at her one day.'

'Perhaps he's a Green.'

'Perhaps.' Le Roy grinned at her, then glanced at his wrist. 'I'd better be off. Look after yourself, Lyra, and if you want anyone eliminated, let me know. For you it would be a favour.'

The door swung shut behind him, and with smooth abruptness Lyra sprang into sudden activity. Pressing the concealed buttons, she attached the hidden instruments to ear and throat. Power surged, died.

'Yes?' whispered the emotionless voice.

'Contact four three nine.'

'Contact four three nine. Proceed.'

'Information on Burgarde. Don Burgarde. Twenty-eight. Single. Local pilot.'

Silence and the soundless surge of hidden power.

'Not known.'

'Give me three eight seven.'

'Contact three eight seven. Proceed.'

'Assassination assignment. Burgarde. Don Burgarde. Twenty-eight. Single. Local pilot.'

A pause, then . . .

'Nothing known.'

'There must be cause. In some way he must be important. Guard him.'

'He will be guarded.'

'Off.'

'Off.'

The surge of power died; the instruments fell silent

For a long moment she sat at the desk, her oddly slanted eyes heavy with thought, then snapping shut the hidden panel, she rose and made her way to where a row of books lined the walls.

One of the volumes opened at her touch, and adjusting the light she commenced rapidly to scan the closely typed pages secreted in the orthodox binding. The Matriarch would have been very interested to see that volume. It contained everything known about her, and a lot that she thought was known to herself alone. From earnest childhood, through adolescence, to maturity, Everyone she had ever been friends with, every little gambit in her rise to power, the enemies she had made, and the friends she had turned into enemies.

For a long time the secretary scanned the flickering pages, then she smiled. Replacing the volume, she turned off the light, swung down a hidden couch, and lying wide-eyed in the darkness, let the turmoil of her brain ease and slow.

From the distant landing field lights flickered as the great strato-liners rose on whispering jets. Clouds gathered, dimming the stars and pouring down a drizzle of rain. Patrolling guards stamped through the wetness, grumbling at the cold damp air.

Once there was the sound of shouting laughter and someone screamed in agony.

Curses mingled with the sound of smashing glass, then boots thudded as the patrols raced to the scene of the disturbance. A shouted command, the thin bark of a high velocity rifle, and silence gathered even more closely around the sleeping city.

★   ★   ★

In her room the Matriarch tossed restlessly on her hard bed, tormented with dreams and frustrated ambition. Figures came to her in the mist-shrouded valleys of sleep. A man's face, then a woman's, they smiled at her, then laughed, then mocked. She muttered a little, heaving her shapeless body on the soft mattress, her thick fingers clenching into fists.

In the outer room, Lyra lay quietly resting, her wide dark eyes staring at the misty haze of the ceiling. Figures arranged themselves in her mind. Production figures, work progress reports, all the thousand pieces of remembered data heard and read during the day. Mentally she plotted a graph, a green line and a red. Very soon now they would touch and then . . .

She smiled and closed her eyes in gentle sleep.

3

Flight

Don Burgarde leaned forward in his seat, cut the engines, and unbuckled his safety belt with a sigh of relief. Above the cabin the great rotors whirled to a standstill, and the chatter of alighting passengers echoed through the thin metal door of the pilot's compartment. He waited until the shrill chatter had died, then followed them onto the warm concrete of the landing field.

He stood for a moment sniffing at the faint breeze, a tall man, with a rangy build and the long flat muscles of hidden unsuspected strength. His hair was blond, cut short and with a tendency to curl. His mouth was wide, with little lines of good humour cut into the tanned skin of his flesh. His eyes were blue, and the firm lines of his nose matched those of his chin. He stood for a moment, then grinned as the relief pilot strode across the field towards him.

'Early aren't you? You're not due to leave for thirty minutes yet.'

'Just thought that I'd check the ship.' The relief pilot grunted, and stared over his shoulder. 'What with things they are, a man's only got to spit and he's looking for work. A crack up would probably earn the death penalty.'

They both laughed, and Don walked slowly towards the field exit. He felt tired, the monotony of the local flights bored him, and the clamping routine seemed to stifle his spirits. His relief had been joking, but what he said was too near the truth for comfort. With the anti-male propaganda that was going on, a man was lucky to have any kind of a job at all. The alternative didn't bear thinking about.

He stopped by the field bar, and entered for a quick drink. Leaning against the polished counter he toyed with his glass, not wanting the drink enough to swallow it, yet not wanting to do anything else. An elbow shoved him rudely aside.

'Get out of the way, *man*!'

A woman glowered at him. A young thing, not more than twenty, but with a hard face, cropped hair, and a sneering arrogance stemming from the certain knowledge that there was nothing he dared do about her actions. She turned to the bar keep.

'Liquor. Quick!'

'Yes, Madam.' The man glanced at Don, made a wry face, and poured the drink. The girl swallowed it, tried not to choke, and glared at them with tear-filled eyes.

'You get many like that?'

'Too many.' The bar tender, an old man, wiped the counter with a wet rag. 'Silly little fools their heads filled with this anti-male propaganda, they come in here trying to ape the male, and think that they can do it by insulting everyone in sight.'

'Talking about me?' snarled the girl.

Deliberately Don turned his back.

'I said are you talking about me?' The girl grabbed at his shoulder, trying to spin him around. She failed, and stepped before him her little face red with anger.

'Nice weather we're having,' Don said pleasantly, and smiled. Deliberately the girl spat in his face.

'Do something about it,' she jeered. 'Go on, do something.'

Hastily Don glanced about him. Several women watched with amusement. one or two men looked uncomfortable but minded their own business. No one was within earshot Carefully Don put his hands behind his back, intertwining his fingers.

'Get away from me you little bitch,' he said softly, 'Or I'll smash your face in.'

She screamed. Staggered back, and appealed to the others. 'He threatened me. He said he'd smash my face in. Guard! Arrest him.'

'Don't be a fool,' snapped a woman. 'He had his hands behind his back, how could he have hurt you?' Roughly she hurried the frenzied girl towards the door. 'Behave yourself, or I'll give you something to remember.'

She returned and smiled at Don. 'Take no notice,' she said. 'What you need is a drink. Whisky?'

'Thanks.' Don accepted the drink and tried not to see the simpering look on her aged face.

'Thank you for standing up for me,' he said with real feeling. 'That girl could have caused trouble.'

'I know it.' The woman stood for a while staring at her drink. 'I don't know what's coming over these young people. Men never acted like that, but these little bits of girls try to act as if they could take on the world single handed.' She smiled. 'Never mind, it's all over now. Have another?'

'My turn,' Don insisted. He pointed towards a table set away from the bar. 'Care to sit?'

'Love to.' Together they settled themselves at the small table.

For a while they sat in silence, Don busy with his own thoughts. Such encounters weren't new to him. There had been other girls swaggering in their arrogance and their desire to show off before a crowd. There had been other women ready to help him out of awkward situations. Sometimes they made an even worse predicament; he hoped that this wouldn't prove the same.

'You needn't worry,' smiled the woman. 'I won't embarrass you.'

He flushed, looking very young and boyish.

'I could read your face,' she explained, 'but I'm not a bar room harpy. I just wanted to help you.'

'Why?'

'Why not?'

They both laughed. Don stretched, feeling a lessening of tension. Casually he stared around the rapidly filling bar: Several people had entered and stood near to where they sat. One woman was arguing in a loud voice.

'I tell you that it is all the fault of the Greens. Why the Matriarch doesn't wipe them out I don't know. Riots, lost production, rumours, all started and caused by those dirty Greens.'

'I wouldn't have thought that they were so dangerous,' protested a man. 'After all their arguments make sense.'

'Isn't that just like a man,' appealed the woman to her listeners. 'Just because they say something he has to believe it. That's just where they are so dangerous. They begin by appealing to the intellect, then they strike at the emotions, before you know it you'll be one of them and there'll be no hope for you.'

'But why should they want to destroy the world,' insisted the man. 'All they say is that it is wrong to build on fertile soil, with the food situation what it is. I should have thought that would have been obvious.'

'There!' The woman looked at her listeners triumphantly. 'What did I tell you? That's the danger of these Greens. He doesn't see that what they want isn't to save fertile soil, but to stop building. Then when we have sunk into anarchy, they'll move in and rule us all.'

'Maybe you're right,' agreed the man helplessly. 'I just didn't think of it that way.'

'You better begin thinking of it like that,' the woman threatened ominously. 'If you don't I'll divorce you. I can always get another husband, but where are you going to get another wife?'

'Not to mention the home, the savings, the car, and the children, chuckled a listener. 'Be a good little boy or Mother will spank.'

The group dissolved in laughter while the man stood with a strained grin plastered to his anger-whitened features.

Disgustedly Don drained his glass, and sat staring at the golden dregs.

'Gets you doesn't it?' murmured the woman. 'All that nonsense about the Greens, I mean.'

'I wasn't thinking of that,' said Don bitterly. 'I was thinking of the man, if he could be called that. Why does he stand it?'

'It's easy to see that you don't love a woman, or more important, that you have no children of your own. A man will stand hell itself for his children, for his wife too, but women are doing a good job of throwing that respect away.'

'And you are a woman?'

'Yes, does that surprise you?' She smiled a little and reached for her glass. 'Not all women are insane, at least not yet. Some of us are still old fashioned enough to know that the old ways had something to commend them. This building on fertile soil, for instance, when we need every square yard for food production. Does it need any great intelligence to see that it is wrong?'

'So you are a Green.' Don rose slowly to his feet. 'Thank you for what you did, but not for your motives. I'd better go now.'

'As you wish, but promise me one thing will you?'

'What is that?'

'Think about it. Think about it a lot.'

'Goodbye,' said Don, and strode from the bar without a backward glance.

Behind him the woman stared sadly at her glass.

A uniformed guard stood at the exit to the field. She wore her black and scarlet with an arrogant air, the slender barrel of her high velocity pistol holstered on her thigh. Beside her stood an official, a sheaf of papers clipped to a board, her eyes bulbous the thick lenses of the spectacles she wore. Both straightened as Don approached.

'Halt! Your name?'

'Burgarde. Don Burgarde. Pilot. Why?'

'One moment.' The official flipped her papers.

'Scheduled as replaceable. Second class pilot local lines.'

'Good enough.' The guard nodded. 'You are reassigned to other labour. Report tomorrow at the labour office. Bring all your papers, and one kilo of personal baggage. That is all.'

'Wait a minute!' he protested. 'What is all this about? What have I done wrong?'

'Wrong? Nothing, you have been assigned to fresh employment, that's all.'

'Is it? What employment?'

'Sea Farm sector seven.'

'No.' He glared at them, his muscles quivering with anger. 'You can't do this to me, I'm not slave labour. I won't go.'

'Suit yourself.' The guard shrugged. 'In any case your employment here is finished. So is every other job. You work at the sea farm or you don't work at all.' She smiled grimly. 'If you're arrested as a vagrant you'll be put to work reclaiming the dead lands. I'd advise you not to be arrested.'

'I'm a pilot,' he insisted hotly. 'I've passed my examinations, it was only a matter of time before I was promoted to the strato-liners. I'm no pick and shovel labourer.'

'You will be,' promised the guard casually. 'Move on, now. Report tomorrow at dawn.'

'Go to hell!' he snarled, and thrust himself past the staring official. A ground car slid past, and he hailed it, slumping angrily in the softly cushioned seat.

'Where to?' asked the driver.

'Central bank, and make it fast will you.' He almost strained his neck beneath the sudden savage acceleration of the turbine-powered car.

At the bank he drew out what funds stood to his credit, it wasn't much. A ground car took him to the modest apartment he shared with his relief pilot, and there he packed what few things he needed. His lips thinned as he stared at the framed certificate hanging on the wall. His first class pilot's licence, unused, and now useless. Irritably he tore it from its frame and stuffed it into his pocket. The ground car still stood at the kerb, the driver grinning at him from the cab.

'I thought that you wouldn't be long. I can always tell a man who's in a hurry.' He swung open the door. 'Where to?'

'Landing field,' said Don absently. 'No, wait.' He frowned. 'Take me to the monorail station.'

They would recognize him at the airfield, and for some reason he didn't want to be recognized. He had broken no law, but he knew how easy it would be to arrest him. A false accusation from some woman, a night in the cells, his money unaccountably vanishing, then either the directed labour or forced to work at reclaiming the dead lands.

The monorail offered a way out. Hastily he purchased a ticket, and impatiently waited for the smooth stream-lined shape to whine along the single rail into the station. The next train was an express, non-stop to the city, and he swung aboard without worrying as to his destination. Anywhere would be better than where he was.

A man grunted as he bumped into him, a man of medium height and medium colouring. He stared at Don with muddy eyes, appearing not to hear the stammered apology, then grunted and sat down in a vacant seat opposite the young pilot. The mono-train jerked, the thin whine of the jet engines cutting the air and vibrating along the metal skin of the streamlined train. Acceleration pressed him deep into the cushions, then as optimum velocity was reached, the pressure vanished.

With only a faint whine from the single rail, the long sleek train plunged across the continent. Don sighed, and looked at his fellow passengers.

The medium-sized man he had bumped into sat opposite, next to him a tall, thin, acid-faced man seemed to be engrossed in a book. A woman stared out of the window, and another sat studying several closely typed pages held in a paper folder. Two other men, medium aged, and both with worried expressions filled the rest of the seats in the compartment. Smoothly the train slid along the single rail, banking slightly at curves but keeping to a steady hundred and fifty kilometers an hour.

A steward moved along the corridor, ringing a little bell.

'Take your place for first dinner please. Take your places for first dinner.'

One of the women rose, smoothing her crumpled blouse. The thin-faced man snapped shut his book, and followed her into the corridor. The plump man with the muddy eyes, yawned, and casually glanced at his wrist.

'Shall we?' he said to Don.

'Why, yes, I'd be happy to eat with you.' Don rose, glad of the company to break the monotony of the journey. 'Are you going far?'

'To the city, and you?'

'The same.' They swayed a little as they walked down the narrow passage leading to the dining compartment, and found a vacant table. For a moment the muddy eyed-man stared at the menu, then grunted as he passed it to Don.

'The usual slosh. Soy bean flower soup. Energised yeast. Vitaminised sea food.

The food on these mono-rails is getting worse each trip.'

'You travel a lot then?' Don asked, politely. He gave his order to the steward, conscious of hunger for the first time since he had come off duty. The man shrugged.

'Too much sometimes, at others not enough. And you?'

'The same.' For a while they ate in silence, spooning the thick soup and tearing at the hard black bread. Outside it was growing dark, the faint glimmer of the setting sun throwing odd shadows across the desolate landscape.

'Almost makes you want to join the Greens doesn't it?' The man gestured towards the windows with his spoon 'Look out there. Sterile soil, the dead lands, and yet we still keep building on farmland. Did you hear of the riot in Central Europe?'

'No.'

'Five guards dead, twenty wounded. The farm workers rioted when the new volcanic power pit was started smack in the centre of a field of wheat.'

'Couldn't they have waited until the grain had been harvested?'

'They don't think like that. The pit was scheduled to be dug, and so dug it had to be.' The man stared out at the darkening night. 'Sometimes I wonder,' he said softly. 'I wonder where it's all going to end. Good land being buried beneath new buildings. The birth rate dropping, and yet still not falling fast enough. The mutants growing up, and more being born every year. The Matriarch encouraging the anti-male laws.' He looked at the young man opposite to him.

'You know, almost I feel sorry for you, a young man, just starting life you might say, and yet with a heritage impossible to bear. A heritage of hate and distrust. A heritage of disease and insanity. If it wasn't for one thing I'd be sorry for you, but grief for the dead is wasted emotion.'

'What?' Don looked at the nondescript figure beside him and tried not to laugh. 'You sound like a Green, and now you sound just plain stupid. I don't need your pity, and believe me friend, I'm a long way from being dead.'

46

'Not so long,' said the man quietly. He held a stylo in one hand and made little doodles on the menu. He stared at Don with his muddy eyes, and his voice was scarcely more than a whisper.

'Your name's Burgarde isn't it? Don Burgarde, single, twenty eight years of age, a local pilot.'

'Ex-local pilot,' Don said bitterly. 'They reassigned me to the sea farms.' He frowned at his fellow passenger. 'How did you know all that about me?'

'I followed you from the airfield. You went to the bank, then home, then raced for the monorail station. I wondered why you were running away, for a moment I thought . . . ' He frowned, then shook his head. 'Never mind what I thought, it doesn't matter now.'

'You don't make sense,' snapped Don irritably. 'Why would you think that I'm going to die?'

'The simplest reason in the world,' whispered the man. He levelled the thick stylo in his hand, as if gesturing to emphasize a point in an argument. 'Tell me about yourself. Why should the

Matriarch want you eliminated?'

'The Matriarch?' Don stared in frank amazement. 'I don't know her, haven't even seen her. You say that she has ordered my death?'

'Yes.'

'There must be some mistake,' decided the young man. 'She can't possibly know me, I couldn't have ever done her harm, and I'm certainly not a danger to her or to anyone.'

'That's what you say.' The man frowned again. 'Tell me, do you know of a woman named Lyra?'

'Lyra? No.'

'That about ends it then.' The man smiled, his round face creasing, his muddy eyes expressionless. 'Goodbye, Don. It won't hurt. It won't hurt at all.'

His thumb tensed on the thick stylo, something spat from a tiny hole in the end, and Don felt the prick of something like a needle in the soft flesh of his throat.

'What?' he gasped. 'What . . . ?'

Darkness edged around him. A great roaring blackness dimming his vision, filling his ears with cotton, cutting off

48

sensation from his arms and legs. Vaguely he sensed a man stooping over him, a thin-faced man with a bitter expression.

'Are you ill? I'm a doctor — are you unwell?'

The stab of a needle registered as the minor prick of an insect, Don gasped, felt the fluttering of his heart, felt his lungs strain for air, then blackness, flame shot, star shot all enveloping blackness.

The thin-faced man stooped over the slumped figure in the seat, then turned to the muddy eyed man.

'Was he a friend of yours?'

'No,' said Le Roy. 'Why?'

'He's dead,' said the tall thin-faced man. 'Heart failure.'

The monorail tore on through the night.

4

Volcanic power

The pit was a gaping sore on the smooth rolling plain. Great piles of valuable topsoil, irreplaceable necessity for cultivation, lay heaped among clay, rock, and debris. Machines had churned the agricultural ground to a muddied mess, and twisted pipe, cable, sections of steel castings, all sprawled for a mile in each direction.

A slim towering building rose from the ground, surrounded by a huddle of rough shacks. A new road twisted through the heaped piles of debris, passed the buildings, and continued to the very edge of the pit. Trucks rumbled along it. Great cargo vehicles, and the smaller tipping trucks, snarling to the edge, to be loaded with crushed rock and soggy clay and then to add their loads to the ugly mounds scattered around.

Men bustled around the pit. Big men, with tired drawn faces, and eyes like burnt-out coals in the whiteness of their faces. Men dressed in a rough grey denim, steel hatted, wearing boots so heavy they seemed to weight listless feet. Surrounding the entire area slender poles supported great floodlights, and further out still, a high wire mesh fence traced a ring about the pit.

Volcanic power pit number seven.

Doctor Moray stood at a window at the peak of the tall slender building, and stared down at the ceaseless activity below. A tall slender man, his sensitive features lined with age and care. A mane of snow-white hair swept back from his high forehead, and his thin, arched nose accented the deep blue of his sunken eyes.

Behind him, from a wide desk, a light flashed red, and a muted buzzer hummed its warning note. Tiredly he crossed the room and flipped a switch.

'Moray here.'

'Report from level nine, sir. Crews report granite.'

'Evacuate, prepare explosive charges, and fire when set.'

'As your order, sir.'

The intercom died, and lines of anxiety deepened on Moray's mobile features.

Around the pit men began to work with a smooth, rehearsed efficiency. The thin cables of elevators whined around their wheels, and crude platforms spilled cargo after cargo of men to the lip of the fifty-foot wide hole. More men followed them, the machines, equipment, all the delicate tools necessary to burrow deep into the Earth's crust. The men disbanded, scurried for shelter, a siren wailed, ceased, wailed again. Delicately the earth shook.

Fumes spouted from the gaping mouth of the pit. Blue smoke, grey, yellow. Fans whirred and the smoke drifted away. Men raced back to the elevators, tugged equipment after them, and were swallowed as the platforms descended. Within minutes after the explosion the scene was as normal.

The intercom hummed its warning note.

'Moray here.'

'Granite shattered, sir. Level nine now completed.'

'Seal levels. No further evacuations. If necessary use explosives adjusted to inter-level firing.'

'As you order, sir.'

'Wait!' Moray hesitated.

'Yes, sir?'

'Any casualties?'

'Three men caught, sir. Five with minor injuries.'

'I see. Carry on.' The power died as Moray opened a curcuit. He passed a trembling hand through the thick white mane of his hair.

A heliojet whined through the air, hovered on spinning blades of glimmering silver, then sank slowly to a perfect landing. Moray watched as the door slid open, then smiled as he recognised who emerged. Impatiently he waited while his visitor checked credentials at the guard station, then waited for the elevator. Barely had it hissed to a halt, than he stood at the door, a broad smile on his thin aristocratic features.

'Lyra! This is a surprise. Why didn't you warn me you were coming?'

'A last minute decision, doctor.' She smiled, and shivered a little, drawing her thick cloak more closely around her slender figure.

'I'm sorry,' apologised Moray. 'I should have remembered your sensitivity to cold, I'll adjust the thermostat.' He swung a control and warmth poured into the room from glowing panels.

'Any news?'

'Nothing of importance,' she smiled. 'I thought that I'd visit you myself so as to give the Matriarch a firsthand report on progress. She is getting a little impatient with the amount of the project's grant. The sea farms are demanding a greater percentage, and the sea farms can promise immediate food production.'

'We offer power, cheap continual power, isn't that enough?'

'No. The Greens are getting more and more troublesome, and not without reason.' Lyra gestured to the window and the scarred landscape beneath it. 'Can you blame them?'

'We can't build without making some sort of a mess. What would you have me do? Tranship the topsoil?'

'Could you?'

'Of course I could — if I had the transport and the time. I don't like waste any more than you do, or the Greens do, but we are working to a time limit, Lyra, you know that.'

'Yes I know that, Moray, and I'm not blaming you, but the Matriarch must be satisfied.'

'The Matriarch!' He swung away and stared out of the window. 'Heaven save me from fanatical women. Men are bad enough. The old time politicians were a case in point, but at least they were human. What would happen if we tried to bribe the Matriarch?'

'Execution.' Lyra was very definite.

'Exactly. Once a woman gets a bee in her head, it's impossible to get it out.' He dropped his hands and turned to face the enigmatic beauty of the secretary. 'What shall we do, Lyra?'

'There is nothing we can do but what we are already doing. The pits must be dug, the power supplied. You know that. There is no other way.'

'I suppose not.' He seemed very tired. 'It is a terrible thing we are doing, Lyra. Have you a conscience?'

'Why do you ask that? Am I a monster?'

'Of course not.' He crossed the room and held her hands, smiling tenderly at her uplifted features. 'I wish that it were all over, and all this worry and struggle done with. It would be so good just to rest.'

'You're tired, Moray. You know as well as I that there can be no rest for any of us, now or afterwards.' She loosened the cloak as the temperature of the room mounted. 'Tell me, why should the Matriarch desire your death?'

'My death?' He stepped back and looked at her in puzzled wonder. 'Does she?'

'She did. I talked her out of it, but the intention was there, and may be there still. Why should she hate you?'

'Doesn't she hate all men?'

'That isn't answering the question.'

'No. No it isn't.' He bit his lip. 'I used to know the Matriarch a long time ago, when she was still young, when we were both still young. We were at the university, and as young people will, pretended that we were in love.' He smiled a little in recollection. 'There was even talk of marriage I believe, but it was towards the end of the peace, and the atom war disrupted everything. We parted, almost I had forgotten about it, and I thought that she had also.'

'She didn't forget. Women never do forget things like that. Forty years and more ago, a long time. Was she beautiful?'

'Beautiful?' Moray frowned. 'I don't know, time dulls so many things. She was pretty, but what woman isn't when she's young and life is full of promise.'

'I see.' Lyra threw off the heavy cloak. 'You may have forgotten, but she never did. I wondered why she should have hated you so, now I understand.'

'But after all these years?' Moray sounded incredulous. 'Surely she would have forgotten by now, or at least forgiven.'

'No. She has a fixation on you, you were her true love, and you let her down. Many women feel like that, especially when they are old and unwanted.'

'But that can't be true!' Moray strode agitatedly about the room. 'She must have forgotten me, she even married, and had a child. How could she persuade herself that her unhappiness is my fault?'

'She what!'

'Didn't you know?' Moray smiled thinly and seated himself at he wide desk. 'It was during the war. She had a sister you know, a normal girl, home loving, maternal but not as pretty as Mary. There was an officer, he married Mary and then divorced her, from what I heard she made his life a hell on earth. That wouldn't have been so bad, but her sister fell in love with the same man. They ran off together, and I suppose that they married after she obtained her divorce. Didn't you know about all this?'

'No. If it all happened during the war it is understandable, most of the records were destroyed, and most of her friends killed. What happened then?'

'Mary had a child, a son, he died three days after birth. In a way it was the best thing that could have happened.'

'Mutant?'

'Yes. Mary had been caught in one of the early raids, the radiation had ruined her as a mother.'

'And her sister?'

'Dead also. She bore a son several years after marrying, a normal child, but the strain killed her.'

'I see. What was its name?'

'The child?' Moray frowned. 'I can't remember. I used to know, but it all happened so long ago. Is it important?'

'Very.'

Moray thought for a while, his delicate features tense with concentration, then he sighed. 'It's no use, I just can't recall the name. I'm sorry.'

'Never mind, it will come to you, and when it does, let me know.'

'I'll do that,' he promised. For a while they sat there, each enjoying each other's company. The intercom hummed its warning signal, and with a gesture of annoyance, Morey flipped the switch.

'Moray here.'

'Curran, engineer tenth level. Look, Doc, can you get down here?'

'Is it essential?'

'Depends on what you call essential,' the voice said drily. 'I've stumbled on something strange. Would you like to see it, or do we smash straight through?'

'How are we keeping to schedule?'

'Time and to spare. I think you should see this.'

'Very well. I'll be right down.'

The power died, and Moray glanced expressively at Lyra. 'I suppose that it's a fossil of some sort, but I'd better take a look. Care to come?'

'May I?'

'Certainly. It is only on the tenth level, about a thousand feet down, and the pressure shouldn't trouble you. I'll phone down and tell them to have suits ready for us.' He smiled. 'At least it will be something to report to the Matriarch.'

The suits were of metal stiffened fabric, designed to prevent minor injuries from falling debris and jagged particles of metal and rock. Muffled in the shapeless suit, with her thick black hair hidden beneath a steel helmet and thick boots on her slender feet, Lyra could almost have passed for one of the diggers. Together she and Moray descended the gaping shaft, balanced precariously on one of the elevator platforms.

'Everything has been sacrificed to speed,' explained the old man as they descended. 'In the old days safety precautions would have been enforced and would have slowed down construction. Now we chance all that.'

'How do the men feel about it?'

'The pay is good, and it is always the other fellow who gets hurt.'

'You sound cynical?' Lyra accused severely. 'Why?'

'Wouldn't you? The labour turnover is more than five percent all due to casualties. Even the simplest precautions have been abandoned.'

A lump of clay disturbed from the rim by a careless foot, thudded onto the platform near to them. Moray gestured expressively. 'See what I mean?'

'But would that have hurt us?'

'Not while we wore the helmets, but that could have been a tool, a piece of rock, anything, and sometimes the men get careless and leave off their helmets. The results aren't pleasant.'

Lyra shrugged and stared interestedly at the steel walls of the pit. Moray gestured towards them.

'We're lining the pits as we dig, it seals the shaft and prevents water seeping through. Usually we do it in one hundred foot levels, but as we go deeper we'll cut the distance. This first part is always the easiest, it's only when we get really far down that the troubles start.'

'Troubles?'

'Cassion disease. Claustrophobia. Heat. A dozen little things. The men have to live where they work, it would take too long to bring them to the surface after each shift. The decompression stages you know. After a while their nerves become frayed and there have been some nasty fights.'

'But surely you fetch them up after a while?'

'Certainly, but to make it efficient they

have to stay below for three months. When they get a break of a week they spend it in town. After that I give them a surface job, then back into the pressure. The turnover mounts to over ten percent when we hit the deep levels.'

The platform jarred to a stop, and carefully they stepped onto a narrow catwalk. Curran, the works foreman, met them, his face glistening with sweat.

'Glad you could come, doctor.' He looked curiously at the shapeless figure of Lyra. Moray didn't bother to introduce them.

'What have you found, Curran?'

'I'm not sure, and yet I've a good idea what it is. This way.'

He led the way along the dirt-covered catwalk, and slipped between the bulk of giant digging machines. A short ladder led to the floor of the shaft, and with a gesture Moray pointed towards a glistening black surface.

'There!'

Moray bent, picked up a fragment, looked at it, frowned, tasted and smelt it, then dropped it with a soft exclamation.

'What is it?' Lyra snapped impatiently.

Moray ignored her. 'Has anyone else seen this?' he asked Curran.

'The usual crew, I stopped work as soon as I guessed what it was.'

'I see.' Moray stood in deep thought for a moment.

'What is it?' repeated Lyra impatiently. Silently Moray handed her a piece of the glistening black substance.

'Well? What is it?'

'You wouldn't know,' Moray said grimly. 'Few people alive now would know, but once it was the commonest mineral found.' He looked at Curran. 'You know what this means if others find out?'

'I can guess,' said the man grimly. He was a thick stocky man with a scarred face and a broken nose. Moray stared intently at him.

'I think that it's about time you were promoted. That is of course, as soon as this level is sealed and the work carried on past this seam. What do you think?'

'I think that it's a good idea,' said Curran. His broken face spread into a grin. 'Don't worry Doc, I can handle my end, if you can handle yours.' He glanced significantly at Lyra as he spoke.

'I can handle it.' Moray sighed and led the way back to the elevator. 'Come on, Lyra. Curran wants to get back to work.'

'But what was it?' insisted the girl. 'What was that black stuff?'

'Coal.' Moray stared blindly at the downward moving walls of the shaft. 'Black diamonds. Political dynamite. Forget it.'

They rode in silence to the top of the pit

5

The Sea Farm

Pain. Pain and the searing agony of returning circulation. Voices muttering in the distance and the unmistakable tang of salt water. Lights blazed at him, and something thudded into his ribs.

'Get up!'

He groaned, struggled upright, and fell back as sickness gripped him. Somewhere a man laughed with evil mirth.

'Better tell those dockside harpies to ease up on the knockout drops. Much more and we'd have a corpse on our hands.'

'Get up you . . . '

Again the boot thudded into his ribs, and with a terrible effort Don sat upright.

'Where am I?' he muttered. 'What's happened?'

'Come on.' A hand gripped his shoulder and wincing with pain he stood unsteadily on his feet. A man glared at him, a big muscular man, with little evil eyes and a thin gash of a mouth. Irritably he shook the swaying figure before him.

'Sleeping time's over, now get to work.'

'Wait a minute Carson, the man's sick.'

'You're too soft,' jeered the big man. 'If you want to wet nurse him, you can, but get him to work by next shift.' He turned, then spun back. 'Listen, Felling, remember I want this man at work, I've stood enough from you and your soft ways, production is dropping, and we need every man.'

His boots rang on the metal of the flooring as he strode heavily away. Felling grinned.

'Take no notice of him, he's tough, but do your best and you'll get on well enough.' He stared curiously at Don. 'What brought you into this?'

'I don't know.' Don staggered a little feeling a supporting arm steadying him. 'What's this all about?'

'You mean that you don't know?' Felling stared at him with enigmatic brown eyes. A tag hung on the front of

Don's jacket, and Felling read it aloud.

'Steve Danton, single, volunteer, contract for five years.' He grinned and dropped the tag. 'Well, Steve, it looks as if you signed on for a five year stretch. You must have been drunk.'

'I wasn't drunk, and my name isn't Danton, it's Burgarde. Don Burgarde, I'm a licenced pilot, local lines.' Memory returned and he frowned. 'At least I was, but they threw me out of my job. I caught a mono-rail, then a man spoke to me and, and . . .'

He frowned as he tried to grasp elusive memories.

'Don't worry about it,' soothed Felling. 'You're here, that's all that matters, and you're going to be here for a long time.'

'No.' Don thrust away the supporting arm. 'Why should I stay? I never asked to come here, and no one can keep me here. Where's the way out?'

'Steady,' warned Felling. He stared at the white faced young man, and his deep eyes narrowed. 'Don't you really know where you are?'

'No.'

'You're at sea farm sector seven,' he said deliberately. 'Now do you remember?'

'I don't remember anything,' snapped Don. 'Not after I spoke to that man on the mono-train.' He swayed a little. 'What's the matter with me?'

'Drugged.' Felling shrugged his mouth bitter. 'They got you the same as they get most of the workers here. A drink spiked with dope. A forged contract, and you're shipped while still in dreamland. Once here there's no way out. You're stuck here, Steve, accept it, and you won't do so bad. Kick, and it's you that'll get hurt.'

'I see.' Don doubled in a sudden fit of retching. 'Got to lie down for a while,' he gasped. 'I'm sick.'

He hardly felt the strong arms of Felling as he was half-carried to a hard bunk. Blackness roared around him, and with the darkness came peace.

Little noises awoke him. The tinkle of coins, the snap and flutter of cards, the occasional sound of gurgling and the hard rap of a glass on the bare wood of a table.

Light streamed over him from a shaded bulb, and the wet smell of the sea was very close.

For a while he lay there, feeling the faint tremor of distant machinery and the soft sough of water circulating through hidden pipes. A shadow fell across his face and slowly he opened his eyes. Felling smiled down at him.

'Better now?'

'I think so.' Don swung himself off the bunk, and licked dry lips. 'Water?'

'Over there.' Felling gestured towards a faucet. 'Help yourself. Hungry?'

'I could manage a meal,' admitted Don with a wry grin.

'I'll get you something, meal break is over but the cook's a friend of mine. How about a sandwich?'

'Perfect.' He hesitated looking up at the enigmatic eyes of his new found friend. 'How about payment?'

'I'll sign a chit, you can pay me later. If I know the dockside harpies, you won't have anything of value left on you. Have a look while I get the food.'

Felling was right. Don examined his

70

pockets and found nothing of value, even his pilot's certificate had vanished. He thinned his lips angrily — the savings of a lifetime gone in a flash. Again he tried to remember his last few moments on the mono-rail.

He looked up as Felling approached, and gratefully accepted the proffered sandwich. It tasted of soy bean flour, the filling being some unrecognisable kind of fish, but his stomach warmed to the needed food.

'Play cards?' asked Felling. 'The boys usually play them off shift; there's not much else to do, and if you can fit in, it will make you popular.'

'I can play, but what about money?'

'Sign a chit with Carson. He'll advance you money against your wages, plus a twenty per cent discount for himself, of course.' Felling shrugged. 'It's the only way. Once you get into debt you stay there, but if you don't borrow, things happen to you — unpleasant things. I'd take the cash.'

'Where will I find Carson?'

'In the office back of the galley.'

'Thanks,' said Don. 'Thanks for everything.'

The slender young man smiled, his deep brown eyes pools of hidden mystery; then turning, he stood casually behind the card players.

Carson looked up with a grunt from where he sat studying a list of figures. He scowled as he recognised Don.

'What do you want?'

'Money. I want to get into a card game. Can you advance me some?'

'Maybe.' The big man looked at him from his little eyes. 'Feel better now?'

'Yes.'

'Willing to work hard?'

'Yes.'

'Good. Some of you people seem to think that just because you arrive here through accident you can loaf through your contract.' He sucked in his lips with a wet hissing sound. 'That's a bad way to look at things, a very bad way.'

'So I gather,' said Don drily. 'Do I get the money?'

'I'll give you eighty and you'll sign for a hundred. Right?'

'Right.' Don pocketed the greasy notes. 'Carson — '

'Yes.'

'How much would it cost to get out of here?'

'Break your contract you mean?'

'Naturally.'

'If you can find someone to replace you, and if you can make it worth the while of certain persons not to look too closely at the new recruit, it might be done.' The big man stared suspiciously at the young pilot. 'You getting ideas?'

'No, just wondering.'

'Well, don't waste your time. It needs outside help and that you haven't got or you wouldn't be here anyway.'

'Thanks for the money, Carson.'

'See that you earn it by working hard.'

'I will. Thanks again.'

The men assembled around the bare wooden table shifted a little as he entered the room, and he squeezed between a runt of a man and one who threatened to sweep him from the bench at any moment.

'Show your money,' the big man

growled, and Don smiled thinly as he spread the greasy notes on the table.

'What are you playing?'

'Stud.'

'Deal me in.'

His first card, the hole card, was an ace. The second a king. He raised the bidding, and sat back to let the game take its course. Three hands and he knew the deal was fixed. Five, and he decided to recapture his losses. It wasn't too hard.

The cheats were the runt of a man and the big man, his secret partner. Their method was simple: merely continue to raise the bidding until the others were forced out. With sufficient money backing them they couldn't lose. It didn't matter what cards any of the others held, they bought each pot by sheer weight of money. Don narrowed his eyes as he saw what was happening, then concentrated on the small man.

It was a trick he had learned when quite small. He could make a man uncomfortable merely by concentrating on him and now he did it to the runt. He shifted uncomfortably, wriggled in his seat, and glanced over his shoulder.

'What's the matter with you?' snarled the big man. 'Your deal.'

'Sorry Ed,' whined the man. 'Your bid.'

Don raised, then raised again. The others dropped out and the two men settled down to their usual practice.

'Raise,' called Don.

'And again,' grunted the big man.

The runt suddenly stood up and walked from the table.

'Call,' said Don.

He stared at the exposed cards and swept in the pot. With a grunt the big man left the table and went after the runt. From outside came a squeal of fear and the soggy sound of a hand smashing into yielding flesh. Don grinned grimly and dealt the cards.

'Wonder what's the matter with Ed tonight?' said a man. He peered at his cards. 'This reminds me of when I used to have a home. My wife was always playing cards. It got so that I had to feed her at the table.'

'What happened?' asked a man, interestedly.

'She lost the lot. I had to work twice as hard but that wasn't what broke us up.'

'No?'

'No. I stood it until she made my boss pay her my wages direct. I had to beg for every penny. That's when I decided to quit.'

'She chase you?'

'What do you think?' snapped the man. 'Of course she chased me, I was her meal ticket. I signed on here to escape being sent to the dead lands.'

'You were lucky,' grumbled a ginger-headed man. He peered at his cards and threw money into the pot. 'What about me? I was having a quiet drink in a bar when a girl comes up and gives me a look. You know how it is.'

A mutter of agreement swept around the table.

'Well, I bought her a drink, then another, and we were chatting away as nice as you please. Then she did it.'

'Did what?' snapped the man who had complained about his wife.

'She said 'Give me money or I'll scream'. Just like that.'

'I know how it is,' nodded a man. 'I was almost caught that way myself. You paid her, of course.'

'No. I was just drunk enough to be obstinate. I threatened to slap her down, and that did it. She screamed, said that I'd insulted her — as if any man living could have insulted her — and before I could move the place was full of guards. At the court next day she claimed that I had made an improper suggestion to her. So help me, I'd done nothing but buy her a drink.'

'Then what happened?' Don leaned forward, thinking of his own narrow escape.

'What happened? They gave me a choice, directed labour or arrest, and you know what that means?'

'The dead lands.'

'Right. I stand a chance of getting out of here alive, but what chance have you got in the dead lands?'

'Tough,' sympathised Felling. 'I know just how you must feel. The way things are a man might as well join up with the Greens.'

A silence fell around the table, a silence so intense that the whimperings of the little runt echoed strangely loud. Someone stirred and cleared his throat with a harsh rasping sound.

'Better pull Ed off the runt or he'll kill him,' he said to no one in particular.

'Better turn in anyway — we've a hard day tomorrow.'

'Some people,' said a man staring hard at Felling, 'just ask for trouble, just beg for it.' He stamped out of the room, the others following him. Felling grinned wryly at Don.

'Well?'

'Well what?'

'Aren't you going too?'

'Why should I?'

'They think that I'm a Green.' He jerked his head towards the door. 'So far no one has tried to do anything about it, but it may not be healthy to seen too friendly.'

'Are you a Green?'

'Are you?'

Don stared at Felling, then shrugged. 'I get it. Each to their own secrets.

Personally, I couldn't care if you were green, blue or yellow.'

Felling smiled.

'An easy way out, but have it your way.' He looked at Don, his eyes flat and glittering faintly in the reflected light. 'I watched you play cards — you knew that Ed and the runt were cheating. How?'

'Did I know?'

'Yes. What did you do to make the runt run from the table?'

'You know too much, Felling. Maybe you know just how I got here?'

'How could I know that, Steve?'

'My name is not, Steve. It's Don. Don Burgarde.'

'As you wish, but hasn't it yet occurred to you that it might be a dangerous name to lay claim to?'

'Dangerous?' Don frowned, then glanced at the young man before him. 'You do know more than you should. What is all this about? Tell me.'

'I know nothing, but think about it for a while. Why should you be sent here? Who hates you enough to sign you on for five years? If you didn't get drunk at some watering tavem, then how did you get here at all?'

'I don't know. I can't remember.' Don looked at Felling. 'What's all this to you? Why should you be interested in me?'

'I have my reasons.' Felling smiled and lowered his voice. 'I believe that we've a lot in common, you and I. A lot in common. Together we could do something about it.'

'About what?' snapped Don. 'What are you getting at?'

'You're young enough, and what you did at the table makes it obvious. Maybe you don't know it, or again maybe you do. I can't blame you for not wanting it known.'

'What?'

'Can't you guess?' Felling's eyes seemed to sink even further into his white face. 'You can trust me, man. Can't you see that? No matter what you say, you can trust me.'

'I don't like this,' snapped Don. He gripped the slack of the loose jacket Felling wore. 'Talk, and talk fast. What are you hinting at?'

'I asked you if you were a Green. I don't think you are.' Felling licked his lips and glanced furtively over his shoulder. 'What if I should ask you something else?'

'Go ahead.'

'Will you promise not to talk about it?'

'Sure, now talk.'

'I think, in fact I'm sure of one thing. I know what you are.'

'That's easy.' Don laughed and thrust the man away. 'I'm human.'

'No,' whispered Felling. 'Not human.'

'Not human?' Red began to tinge Don's pale face.

'No.' Felling swallowed, then began to talk with desperate earnestness. 'I know how you must be feeling, but try not to let it upset you. You aren't the only one, there are thousands just like us. Hiding, afraid to declare ourselves, miserable and insecure. We've got to get together, stand by each other, and demand our rights.'

'You said that I wasn't human,' insisted Don. What am I?'

'A mutant,' whispered Felling. 'You're just like me. A mutant.'

'You're joking.' Don shook the man by

the slack of his jacket. 'You must be joking. Do you realise what you're saying, man? Tell me that this is your idea of fun. Tell me!'

'Don't!' whimpered Felling. 'You're hurting me.'

'Then say it,' snapped Don. 'Damn you, say it! I'm human, aren't I? As human as you or anyone else! I'm no monster, no spawn of atomic disruption. I had normal parents, a normal birth, a normal life. Why do you call me a mutant?'

'I could tell from what you did,' babbled Felling. 'I could sense it, I can sense these things — don't ask me how or why, I just can!'

'You're crazy!'

'No, not crazy.' Felling drew himself up with a sudden quiet dignity. 'I'm what I am. I didn't ask to be born, neither did you. We're both of us the same. Both mutants.'

Don smashed him in the mouth.

6

Sea harvest

Work started all too soon. Carson hustled them into a steel room, reeking of damp and smelling of salt. He jerked a thumb at Felling, and grinned at the man's swollen face.

'What's the matter, Felling? Your girl friend kiss you too hard?'

A burst of rough laughter echoed from the other men assembled in the suit room, and Felling flushed.

'Well, get to work. You take charge of the new hand, the rest of you know what to do. Now get out there and don't come back until your air's exhausted. If you do, I'll send you straight out to serve another shift.'

Grimly the men donned their armour, Felling helping Don with the stiff metal of the unfamiliar suit.

'Stay close to me,' he muttered as he

clamped the headpiece. 'I'll show you what to do.'

Carson stamped around the room checking their suits and seeing that each man held his combination cutter and rake. Satisfied, he stepped back from the room, slammed the thick inner panel, and operated the valve. Water gushed into the room.

Don swallowed, trying to control his fear. The water boiled through the valve tugging at his limbs and dashing against the faceplate of his helmet. The flow ceased, and he felt a tug as Felling jerked his arm. Together they stumbled from the room and on to the seabed.

'Stay close to me!' The voice echoed thinly through his helmet, and he knew that Felling had placed his own headpiece against the one he was wearing. Sound, carried by conduction, was the only method of communication possible without radio.

'In a way we're lucky. All this portion of the seabed has been cultivated for a long time. It only gets bad in the deeper levels and we won't go there for a long time.'

'What do we have to do?'

'Rake away any other growths between the main patches. Cut all weed over three feet high, bundle it and lay it in the path. We'll collect it on the way back. If you see any fish or crustaceans, catch them and immobilise them. To work now.'

Don watched his guide for a moment then gripping his tool in both hands set to work. It was harder than it looked. The water resisted every movement, exaggerating the slightest gesture. The suits were heavy, and soon his muscles ached as he stumbled blindly over the seabed swinging the heavy cutter. Once he stumbled, and before he could prevent it, he had fallen full length in a patch of the thick seaweed that was the produce of this 'farm'. In momentary panic he threshed and struggled to regain his feet. The weed tangled his limbs, slipped from beneath his feet obscured his helmet. In blind panic he threshed helplessly, tangled in interlaced weed.

Something gripped his belt, and thankfully he felt the tangled weeds release his limbs.

'Take things easy for a while,' whispered Felling. 'Try not to rush things. Let the weight of the cutter do the work. Remember, you are fighting water resistance, and you've got to allow for that.'

'How much longer does this shift last?' gasped Don.

'About three hours. Why?'

'I'm all in.' Weakly Don sagged in Felling's grip. 'I never thought it would be like this. Working under water should be easy.'

'It would be, if you didn't have to wear a suit, if you didn't have to swing a ten-foot cutter, and if you didn't have to carry around two hundred pounds of lead.' Felling sat on the cleared seabed between the cultivated patches, gestured to Don to join him. Their helmets rang slightly as Felling made contact.

'We're about sixty feet down, hardly any depth at all. The real trouble starts when you get about a hundred and fifty.'

'Do they cultivate that deep?'

'Yes.' Felling sounded bitter. 'Sector seven has over two square miles at that level. Now the orders are to go even deeper.'

'Why?'

'The Matriarch is desperate for increased food production. I heard Carson telling one of the foremen that we're to tackle the two hundred plus level.'

'Is that bad?'

'What do you think? Working with pressurized suits, operating by the thin light of portable searchbeams. The seabed is rough out there, and the currents are deadly. Larrimie Deep is only a quarter mile further out. The bed drops sharply when you leave the coastal shelf. Once in the Deep and you're a dead duck. We've lost ten men that way as it is.'

'Then why do they try to cultivate so far out?'

'What else can they do? Every square mile of land is cultivated. The fishing fleets are scouring the seas, and the yeast plants and hydroponic farms are working at full pressure. Still we haven't enough food. What else can we do but farm the sea bottom? There is enough land beneath the sea to supply the entire world with food. The only thing is it's too hard to cultivate. We clear a stretch, plant mutated seaweed with a high vitamin and protein content. We let it grow, and lop off the excess growth. The cheapest form of farming there is, and yet the most dangerous.'

'I don't quite get this,' argued Don. 'As I remember history, they used to have enough food from normal farming methods. Why can't we do the same?'

Felling chuckled, his thin laugh echoing through the helmet.

'Why? Well, first the cities were atom bombed, and they to build new cities. Then the arable lands were dusted with radioactives, and those lands are now sterile. That cut down the available land by about a quarter. Then natural minerals ran out, oil, coal, forests, peat. We had to grow crops to replace the lost oils and raw materials. That means that a tremendous amount of land is devoted to mechanistic requirements. Castor oil plants, cotton, hemp, a dozen others, all needed for oils, cellulose, the raw materials for plastics. All taking a tremendous amount of room, but none of it used for food.'

'But what else could we do?' Don stirred restlessly in the cramped confines of his suit. 'Civilisation must progress. Do you want us to go back to horse transport?'

'We couldn't even if we wanted to — there simply aren't enough horses. No. That isn't the answer.'

'Then what is?'

'For a start we could stop building runways ten miles long for the stratoliners. We could build new houses on useless ground, or better still, build them higher. We needn't rip up valuable topsoil when sterile ground is available. In short, we could use a little sense and save what we've got.'

'That's just the way the Greens talk,' snapped Don. 'You told me that you were not a Green.'

'Did I?' Felling laughed quietly. 'I don't remember. Even if I am a Green, does that make the truth any less truthful?'

'Propaganda,' said Don. 'Lying propaganda. I admit that what you say makes some sort of sense, but you haven't told me everything. The Greens are clever — they state a truth, then cover it with lies. They say stop building on agricultural ground, but what is their alternative?'

'Isn't it obvious?' Felling paused, stabbing at the sandy bottom with his long cutter. 'What about atomic power?'

'Are you insane?' Don stared at the grotesque figure hunched beside him. 'Hasn't the world had enough of atomics? What of the dead lands? The blasted cities? Yes, and what about the mutants? Do you want to destroy the world utterly? Once was enough, once was almost too much. Now I know just how dangerous the Greens are. Atomic power! Not while I'm alive and can use a gun.'

'Spoken like a true unthinking patriot,' Felling sneered, bitterly. 'Did the first man who made fire refuse to repeat the experiment because he burnt himself? Did the first man to ride a horse give up because he fell off? Did you commit suicide when you first failed to walk? Of course you didn't — why should you? And why should men deliberately refuse the benefits of atomic power?'

'The warning is all around us,' Don said grimly. 'Your analogy isn't correct. To play with atomics is to endanger the world. We have proved that.'

'We have proved that a tool is only as useful as its user, a discovery only as potent as we wish. Atomics were born during a war, and naturally were used as a weapon. But there was an interim period, a time of peace. Atomic research did not stop at making bigger and better bombs. Atomic power piles were built, small, safe, self-governing. It is impossible for a well-designed pile to explode, impossible by the very nature of its self-contained safety margin. Not one atomic power pile ever exploded, or did any more damage than superficial burns to attendant personnel.'

'Look at the world,' jeered Don. 'The scars of atomics are everywhere.'

'And so are the scars of fire, but we still like to keep warm,' snapped Felling. 'I tell you we have no choice: If civilisation is to progress, and unless it does progress we shall sink into decadence and the darkness of ignorant superstition, then we must have power. Atomic power. There is nothing to take its place, no alternative we can use. Atomic power or a new dark age. Which would you prefer?'

'I don't know,' muttered Don. 'I've seen what atomics can do. Maybe a breathing space is what we want, a time to stop and think things over. Would another dark age be terrible?'

'I don't know. Perhaps it depends on what you mean by 'terrible'.' Felling sighed. 'Better cut some weed now. Carson expects us to fill a quota.'

Painfully Don climbed to his feet, and began swinging the long cutter. The light was dim, filtering down through sixty feet of water, and he could see for a few yards in each direction, beyond that, things grew vague and unreal.

Mechanically he worked. Swing, turn so as not to fight the water resistance, then swing again. The tangled fronds of weed accumulated around him, and clumsily he lashed them into bundles with short lengths of twine. Hours passed. His arms grew heavy, his muscles shrieking with agony at every motion.

Sweat ran down his forehead, stinging his eyes and searing his tender skin where the harsh fabric of the suit had rubbed it raw. He gasped for breath, his lungs a burning agony. Still he worked.

Something vibrated through the water. A pulsing, a shaking. More of motion than of sound. It was repeated, then again, and yet a fourth time. Wonderingly, Don halted, staring blindly about him. The bloated figure of a worker rode with carefully exaggerated steps towards him, the faint clang as their helmets touched seeming very loud.

'The recall signal,' explained Felling. 'Work your way back to the station, raking the weed as you go.'

Don nodded, forgetting that the gesture was a waste of motion, and began to follow the other's example, dragging the great masses of bundled weed behind him as he returned along the cleared path between the cultivated patches.

It was hard work. The bundles had a tendency to drift away, and the long rake grew heavier by the minute. Don was on the point of utter collapse when the rounded dome of the station came into sight.

Carson met them, looming huge in his suit. He stood by the loading port, and checked each man's quota, marking the figures on a slate. Don rested on his cutter as he waited his turn.

Most of the men, he noticed, had a far larger quantity of weed than he did. Some of them seemed to have more than twice as much. Despondently, he glanced at his own pile, and then stiffened in sudden anger.

A man stood almost out of vision at the edge of the pile. A huge bulking man, looking like some mediaeval giant in his suit and with a long lance-like cutter. Even as Don watched he deliberately raked a bundle from the pile and threw it behind him with a practiced gesture. A smaller man, almost a dwarf beside his companion, grabbed hold of the weed and added it to a huge pile. Instinctively Don strode forward, lifting the cutter as he did so.

He stopped. It was useless, no coward, yet he knew himself too near exhaustion to even think of battle in an unfamiliar environment where the slightest damage to his suit would result in immediate and unpleasant death. He stood fuming, as the huge man calmly helped himself to several more bundles.

Carson gestured towards him, and awkwardly Don raked his pile of weed into the loading port. The overseer counted them, checked the weight, and gestured for Don to enter the sally port. Other men followed him, the outer door swung shut, and air hissed into the compartment, expelling the water.

Within minutes Don had thankfully divested himself of the cumbersome suit, and rubbing aching limbs followed the others into the dining hall. They sat around for a while waiting for the rest of the shift, Don glaring at the huge Ed and his little runtlike friend.

'Something wrong?' snarled the big man.

'You should know,' snapped Don.

'What are you getting at?' Ed pushed back his chair and towered over the slighter man.

'Nothing.'

'Then don't look at me like that. I don't like it.'

'Maybe you don't, and I don't like having you steal my weed.'

A silence fell on the group sitting at the table. Felling started to his feet, another man pulling him down. Ed glanced about him, then leaned forward, his gross face ugly.

'Just what are you getting at?'

'If you don't know then I'm not telling you,' snapped Don. Hw tried to control his rising anger. He knew that he was in no condition to do battle with the huge man.

'You said something just then, something I don't like,' said the big man softly. 'If you think I stole your weed, why don't you complain to Carson?'

'Would that do me any good?'

'Try it and see.' The big man laughed scornfully. Deliberately he pressed the palm of his huge hand against Don's face and pushed. His strength was incredible. Don fell off his chair and slid halfway across the room. Red-faced he regained his feet, as a chorus of sniggers came from the watching men.

'You big ape!' Don grabbed at the chair and threw it. He followed the missile, fists pumping at the sneering face. Something smashed into his mouth, something else thudded against his jaw. The lights reeled and he could taste the warm saltiness of blood. Dimly he saw the big man raises his fist.

'Hold it!' roared a voice. Carson stood in the doorway, legs straddled eyes glowering beneath bushy brows.

'Hold it I say.' He glared at Don. 'Danton, come into the office, I want to talk to you.' He glared at the big man. 'I've warned you before about fighting. Now stop it.'

He turned away.

7

Battle

Carson sat at his scarred desk of unpolished wood, and stared at Don. His beefy face and narrow eyes watched as the young man wiped the blood from his split lips, and tried to control his anger. The overseer grunted, and gestured towards a chair.

'Sit down.'

'Thanks,' gasped Don. He looked at Carson. 'What do you want with me?'

'First, your quota wasn't enough, nowhere near enough. What had you been doing? Talking? Asleep? Looking at the scenery?'

'I did my best,' snapped Don. 'Remember that I'm not used to this work, you can't expect me to gather as much as the older hands.'

'I'm not interested in excuses!' Carson slammed his fist down onto the rough table, 'I expect every man here to gather his quota, if they don't, then there are ways of persuading them.' He grinned without humour. 'Some of those ways are quite effective.'

'I did my best,' said Don. 'I lost several bundles while waiting to check in.'

'I can't help that,' snapped the overseer. 'Your personal quarrels have nothing to do with me.' He stared at the young man. 'You don't like it here do you?'

Don smiled, not answering.

'You don't have to tell me,' grinned Carson. 'I know your type. Soft, that's what you are. Better suited to acting as a lady's maid than to doing real men's work. Well I've a proposition to put to you, one that should suit your special requirements.'

'Yes?'

'I can you out of here, medical grounds, get you a shore job or one in the office, maybe even a pilot's job. We have our own transport you know.'

'What's the catch?'

'No catch. I've noticed that you and

Felling seem very close. I'm glad of that, I've tried to get a man near to him for a long while now. It looks as if you are the one.'

'Yes?'

'I think Felling's a Green.' Carson stared intently at Don. 'Do you like Greens?'

'No.'

'I thought not. No sane man could, and you seem sane enough.'

'What's the proposition?'

'I've just told you. If Felling is a Green, and you could join them — learn all about them — who is in charge of the local group and other things, then I'll get you an easy job.'

'And if he is a Green, what happens to him?

'What do you think? He and all his friends go to forced labour in the dead lands.' Carson grinned. 'I'd like to kill him personally, but the dead lands will do it for me, and do it in a very unpleasant manner.'

'Why are you interested in catching Greens?' Don looked shrewdly at the big overseer. Carson laughed.

'I thought that you had brains. Why I want to catch them in my business. I've told you what you can expect out of it.'

'Promotion — and you would get even bigger promotion.' Don nodded. 'It makes sense. For a moment I was afraid that you'd gone patriotic.'

'What I get out of it is my business,' snapped Carson. 'Well?'

'I don't like it.'

'You'd like forced labour in the deep levels better?'

'No.'

'Then you'll do it?'

'Have I any choice?'

'None.' Carson laughed and held out his hand. 'Shake on it. Get near to Felling, get him talking, join his group, you know what to do. You'll never regret it.'

'But what if he isn't a Green,' protested Don. 'What then?'

'He's a Green,' snapped Carson. 'If he isn't now, he will be when you testify against him. What does it matter?'

'Nothing,' admitted Don. 'Call a man a

101

Green and he's as good as convicted. All I need to do is to invent some conversations, swear that he tried to convert me, and I can't go wrong. Simple.'

'I knew that you had sense,' grinned Carson. He rose. 'Get back to the recreation room now. I'll have a word with Ed. He won't bother you again. How much weed do you think he stole off you?'

'At least five bundles.'

'Call it ten,' suggested Carson. 'I'll dock his pay and credit it to your name. Get busy now. We haven't much time.'

Don nodded, and left the office. He felt very sick.

* * *

Silence, and darkness, and a voice whispering in his ear. Don rested on the hard bunk staring at the invisible ceiling, and listened to the swift words of a desperate man.

'What are you going to do, Don? Are you going to report me? You know what it means if you do?' Felling sounded on the verge of hysteria.

'Relax,' warned Don. 'I've told you what Carson said to put you on your guard. If I don't report you, someone else will. You're a marked man, Felling. Better do some quick thinking.'

'But what can I do? If I were a normal man I could handle this thing but I'm not. I told you: I'm a mutant. I've a different nervous system to other men. I can't stand pain — I'll say anything they want me to, to avoid it. What can we do, Don?'

'How do you mean — we?'

'You're a mutant too, remember. If Carson doesn't succeed with me, he'll try you next. We haven't got a chance,'

'You've a short memory, haven't you, Felling? Remember the last time you called me a mutant?'

'You hit me, but I don't blame you for that. You couldn't help it. It was due to your years of conditioning. You have been taught to believe that all mutants are things of horror, monsters, things with twisted limbs, and freakish bodies. Mutants aren't always like that, Don. Some of them are as human appearing as you and I.

We're different in little things — a slight alteration of the blood perhaps, a subtle difference in the manner in which we think. That's why most of the Greens are really mutants. They are able to see things so much more clearly than the normal person. A mutant isn't blinded with fear and hysteria as humans are. You must help me, Don, for in helping me you will be saving yourself.'

'Then you are a Green?'

'Of course I'm a Green. So are you if you'd only stop to think about it.'

'You take a lot for granted,' whispered Don coldly. 'You fall into a very common error, I'm not what you want me to be, merely because you want it. I am an individual with my own concepts of right and wrong. I've warned you because I don't like playing the traitor. Because I warned you, it doesn't mean that I am bound to help you.'

'You will help me though.' Felling sounded strangely confident. 'I am going to help you, and then you will help me. Listen. Ed, the big man, is coming to kill you.'

'Is he?'

'Yes. I can read it in his mind. I don't know just how or when. He hasn't decided that yet, but he has decided to eliminate you. He blames you for docking his pay. Carson warned him about stealing weed, and he thinks that you told the overseer about him.'

'I didn't,' said Don.

'He thinks that you did.'

'Well, what can I do about it? If he's decided to kill me now, he may have altered his mind by tomorrow. Why should he kill me? What harm can I do to him?'

'If you wanted to, quite a lot. Remember how you made the small man leave the table? I caught the backwash of your directed concentration then, and if you would only develop that talent, you could kill by your mental power alone.'

'Nonsense!'

'Is it? What is thought? An electrical disturbance of the mind. Well, what you do is to upset the measured rhythm of a thought pattern. You create a condition of mental stress by heterodyning the wave pattern of normal thought. The subject is disturbed: how could he be otherwise? He cannot think properly, and doesn't know what is happening to him. That, Don, is your mutant power.'

'And I could kill with it?'

'Certainly. You could interfere with normal thought so much that the subject would literally forget to live. His heart would stop, his breathing. He would die and never know what caused his death.'

'Interesting,' said Don drowsily. 'Get some sleep now, I'm tired.'

'I never sleep. I never have slept. All I can do is lie and think and rest. There is something different in my brain that makes sleep unnecessary. That is my mutant power. That, and a high degree of telepathic awareness.'

'Rest then. I'm tired, I must sleep.'

'Will you help me?'

'Tomorrow. I'll think of something tomorrow.'

Don drifted into the sleep of sheer exhaustion.

It was bad the next day. His muscles, still sore and aching, hardly permitted him to swing the heavy cutter. The day after was a little better, and within a week he had recovered his strength. Carson treated him gently, the huge Ed distantly, and the other men gradually accepted him as an equal. If it had not been for Felling, Don would have been content to let things slide. The work was hard, but it was man's work. The food was good and plentiful, the other men rough but human. After shift they played cards, drank sparingly of forbidden liquor, or stared at the telescreens with their romantic plays, girl shows, and more increasingly, scenes of the ascendancy of the feminists. Such shows resulted in ribald mirth from the hard-bitten workers, and lewd suggestions to the severe faced women portrayed on flickering screens.

One woman caused whistles of undisguised admiration. Lyra, secretary to the Matriarch, explaining the terrible importance of the volcanic power project, aroused feelings quite different from the other speakers. She spoke calmly, and yet with a burning intensity which created a desperate need to assist in any project in which she was interested. Don didn't realise it, but she was the only speaker who deliberately used the weapons of her sex to convince her male viewers.

The Matriarch, her harsh face stern and set, won the feminist element to her way of thinking. Between them they had convinced nearly all the world that the volcanic power pits meant the future well-being of the world.

Felling smiled a little as he listened to the hum of conversation following the broadcast. Ed, his big coarse features twisted in unthinking rage decided that the slight man was grinning at him. In seconds Felling lay in a cot, blood streaming from his nose, and Ed was fighting mad.

'You pasty faced scut!' he roared. 'Laugh will you? By hell's gates I'll make you laugh the other side of your face. Get up damn you! Get up I say!' His heavy boot swung, swung again. Felling screamed in agony, doubled up as the boot smashed into his ribs.

Don sprang forward.

He forced himself to remain calm. In any brawl he was certain to lose to the superior weight and strength of the big man. He must use science, cunning, guile. Savagely he kicked the big man in the knee, sank his fist low into the stomach, and stepped back just in time to avoid a blow which would have pulped his skull like a rotten orange.

Ed whined with animal rage and pain. He limped a little, but his little eyes burned with insane fury. He flexed his huge hands, stepped forward and brought up his knee in a vicious blow to the groin.

Don twisted, feeling his thigh grow numb as it received the impact of the blow. He struck with the edge of stiffened hand at the big man's thick throat, missed, and desperately covered with his other arm. Lights blazed before his eyes, and as from a terrible distance he heard man's shrill cry.

'Blind him, Ed. Go for his eyes.'

Something smashed into his face, and he felt the quick warm flow of blood. Desperately he broke away from the huge man, fighting for breath and feeling fear for the first time.

He couldn't win!

The big man could take all the punishment he was capable of delivering and still retain sufficient strength to maim and cripple, Don had no doubt as to what would happen to him. They weren't fighting to rules. There was no code of honour. It was hurt or be hurt. Cripple or be crippled. Kill or be killed. No tactic was too dirty, no strategy too vile but that it couldn't be used.

Cautiously he braced himself for the next rush.

It came in a shower of blows, in a rain of thrusting knees and swinging boots. Don weaved, twisted, jabbed with the stiffened fingers of his hand, slashed with the hard edge, and struck with the full power of arm and shoulder muscles. He felt something yield beneath the cutting blows of his right hand. Quickly he repeated the blow to the exposed throat, thrust with his left thumb at the unguarded eye, and threw several blows into the pit of the stomach.

Ed retched grunted, and lashed out with his heavy boot. Pain flooded from

Don's shin. Terrible searing pain, bringing tears to his eyes and a horrible sickness to his stomach. The big man grinned, mrasured his distance, and deliberately kicked him in the pit of the stomach.

The world exploded into a hell of bloodstained agony.

Don dropped, bent double, hands clutching his injuries. Dimly he was aware of boots, crashing into his exposed ribs, and the frenzied yells of the watching men. Numbly he knew that the big man intended to break his ribs, puncture his lungs, cripple and maim him for life. His body was useless, too tormented with pain to obey his desperate mental commands. He had only one thing left.

Grimly he forced himself to concentrate, to cease wondering about his stricken body, to block out the pain and the fear. Sweat started on his forehead, and his ears hummed as from a giant top, but still he concentrated. If Felling had been right, he still had a chance, if wrong, then nothing mattered much anyway.

The blows ceased. From the watching

men rose a murmur then a drone of puzzled wonder, finally a shout.

'What's the matter?'

'Gone soft, Ed?'

'Finish him now, what are you waiting for?'

Dazedly Don looked at the big man.

He stood wide legged, a stupid expression of his heavy features, a blank expression, an idiot look. He swayed, half lifted his foot, then dropped it and stared wonderingly at the assembled men. Grimly Don struggled to his feet. The big man might be unwilling to fight now, but how long he could hold the terrible mental concentration was doubtful. Also he was human enough to desire revenge.

His fist pulped the broken nose. His stiffened hand lashed across the exposed throat, and his boot crashed into a knee. The big man shook his head, grinned stupidly, then suddenly broke into berserk fury. Coldly Don smashed blow after blow into the rage-maddened animal before him. Twice the big man tried to kick him in the groin. The third time Don stepped back, grabbed at the extended boot, twisted and heaved. With a crash that made the light bulbs dance in their sockets, the big man fell to the steel floor plates.

He lay half stunned, his little eyes glazed. Don stepped back, watching him cautiously.

'Had enough?'

'Help me up,' grunted the fallen man.

Don stepped forward, extended his hand, then leapt high into the air to avoid a vicious kick.

'You asked for it,' he said grimly, and swung his foot. It was a well-judged blow, not too hard to cause permanent damage, but hard enough to render the great figure of the fallen man helpless. Ed sighed, then slumped, a thin trickle of blood rilling from his temple.

'Finish him!' yelled a man. 'Kick him to pieces. He would have done it to you.'

'No,' gasped Don. He swayed a little feeling the pain from his stricken body burn along his nerves.

'Was it a fair fight?'

'Yes!' roared the men.

Don grinned, then stumbled to his bunk. The workers were rough, but they would prevent any more trouble. It was their only code of conduct.

8

Escape

The water was green and cold and surged with unexpected currents. The tall fronds of cultivated weed swayed and writhed beneath the surging water, and the darting bodies of small fish interlaced the dark green plants with flashes of silver. High clouds had cut the surface light, hiding the sun, and turning the undersea farm into a place of dim mystery.

Don frowned, trying to penetrate the murk, narrowing his eyes and thrusting his face close against the transparent face piece of his helmet. The long cutter in his bare hands swung in a lazy arc and severed fronds of weed drifted slowly to the bottom. He stooped, gathered them into a bundle, and lashed them with weighted twine. He walked slowly along the cleared path between the cultivated patches, cutting and tying as he went, working automatically, his thoughts busy on past events.

Carson was growing impatient.

He had spoken in no uncertain terms about the lack of progress Don had made, and hinted that unless Felling was reported as a Green, both of them would be accused by some other. Don had little doubt that their accuser would be the giant, Ed.

Since the fight, the big man had kept well away from him, but the look in his little eyes whenever they met warned the young pilot what to expect if he should ever get careless. He shrugged, swung the cutter in a wide arc, interestedly watching the keen blade slice through the tough stalks of the thickly growing weed.

He wondered what the Matriarch would do when all the coastal shelves had been cultivated. Probably attempt floating farms, similar to the one growing in the gulf stream. Not all types of seaweed could be processed and made edible, but certain varieties could be used for valuable vitamins. He shrugged again, and idly stabbed at a cruising fish. The silver body avoided the slowly moving point with ease, and returned to browse on the prolific growth.

A shadow moved at the extreme range of vision. A hulking something bearing a long lance-like cutting tool. Don frowned, squinting his eyes. Felling shouldn't be due at this point for another quarter hour. He raised an arm in greeting.

The shadow moved closer, hefting the cutter. Don frowned. This was too big for Felling, too big for any man except . . .

He ducked as the razor edge of the cutter swept through the water where he had been standing.

'What are you trying to do?' yelled Don, forgetting that the sound couldn't be heard.

The figure moved closer.

Instinctively Don guarded with his own tool. The long knives clashed, almost tearing the handle from his hands. He cursed, stepped back as rapidly as he could, and saw the sharp point of the other's weapon coming straight towards him.

Desperately he sidestepped, then as he

saw the point following him, parried with his own cutter. For a while they stood in a clumsy parody of two fencers, thrusting, parrying, slashing and dodging, but there would be nothing funny about the results if one of the razor edges struck home. A tiny slit in the tough fabric of the suits, and water would thrust into the opening, bringing certain death by drowning.

Don spun slowly, cursing the water that made every movement a thing of slow motion. Superior agility was wasted here. Experience and brute strength would be the determining factors of this strange battle. Grimly he concentrated, bringing the full weight of his newly discover mental powers to bear on his opponent.

A razor edge licked towards him, skidded from the haft of his own weapon, and traced a thin red line across the back of his hands. Jerked into caution, Don shortened his grip on the long handle of the cutter, and stabbed at the grotesque figure before him. The point struck against one of the broad chest weights, the brittle steel snapping beneath the impact.

Even as he twisted to avoid a backhanded slash, Don reasoned why his mental powers were useless. The metal of the helmets plus the body of water between them, must have absorbed his mental force. Not that it mattered. Explanations could come later. Now, action was essential.

He slipped, fell to one knee, and saw the black bulk of the suited worker lift his weapon for a destroying slash. Kicking against the soft bottom, Don threw himself forward, threw himself to the very edge of the tangled weed. A shadow passed his face plate, and a numbing shock made him gasp with fear. The blade had struck the belted weights around his waist, and before the big man could set himself for a second blow, Don had regained his feet. Grimly he stood waiting, the broken cutter poised before him, one hand busy at the fastenings of his belt.

For a moment the big man hesitated, half lifting his long weapon as if to throw it like a spear, then realizing the foolishness of such a move, began to stride deliberately forward. Don tensed, holding his cutter as if it were a foil, ready for the thrust or slash he knew must come. The big man stepped closer.

His attack was simple, fast, and could have been deadly. A feint with the point, a second with the edge, then the long weapon slid in a smooth arc directly at Don's stomach. He tensed, swung his own weapon, parrying the thrust and forcing the point away from his body. He lunged forward, using his cutter as a barrier between himself and the razor edge menacing him. Desperately he kicked at the soft sand, thrusting himself forwards through the binding water. He dropped his cutter, swung his hand in a long arc, and came within touching distance of his enemy's face plate. One glimpse he had of rage-distorted features, of little glaring eyes, and a writhing mouth, then the belt weight smashed into the brittle glass and shattered it to glittering ruin.

The big man died, his mouth gasping for air, his eyes wide in sudden fear. He died, and bubbles rose in a continuous stream from the shattered helmet. He died, and Don felt the nerve-quivering shock of reaction. Mechanically he closed the valve on the dead man's helmet, and tried not to see the distorted features framed in the gaping hole.

A hand gripped his shoulder.

Startled he spun on his heel, the heavy weight from his belt raised and ready to strike. Felling stared at him, then at the dead man. Urgently he gestured and their helmets clashed together.

'What have you done?'

'I killed him. He attacked me, and I had to defend myself.' Don paused. 'What do we do now?'

'I don't know.' Feeling breathed heavily the sound echoing through the helmets

'How far is to shore?' demanded Don.

'To shore, I'm not certain, but it can't be very far, we're only sixty feet deep.'

'That means nothing,' snapped Don. 'With a gentle slope from the shore, sixty feet could put us over ten miles out.' He kicked at the dead man. 'Better get rid of him I suppose, it may slow down pursuit.'

'Are you going to make for shore?'

Felling sounded anxious.

'Yes, and if you have any sense you'll come with me. Carson is getting anxious for a scapegoat. He warned me that unless I accused you of being a Green, he'd accuse us both. If you want to stay and face it, you're welcome, but I'm getting out while the going's good.'

He bent and unscrewed the air flask from the dead man's suit, then remade contact.

'Help me throw him into the centre of that weed. It'll take time for them to find him there, and we need time. Ready now?'

Together they lifted the bulk of the dead man and thrust him deep into the tangled fronds. Don threw the broken cutter after him, and stood in sudden doubt.

'Felling. Which way is the shore?'

'That way. The deep levels lie over there, and the shore should be further back.'

'Good. You lead the way and avoid the station. Try not to meet any others, or if you do, pretend we're on normal business. Ready?'

'Yes.'

'Any questions?'

'No.'

'Good. Let's get moving.'

Together they strode through the dim water, each step an exaggerated movement, slow and deliberate, as they thrust themselves through the hindering water. Fish darted around them, staring at the strange monsters with goggling eyes. Little drifts of suspended sand obscured their face plates, and the steady hiss of air from their tanks mingled with the harsh sounds of their breathing.

Carefully they wended their way through the patches of cultivated weed, past the squat dome of the station, then into an area of broken rock, slippery with algae and jagged with the discarded shells of limpets and barnacles, periwinkles and oysters. Felling stumbled, scratching his hands badly on the jagged shards, Don pulled him to his feet, and supported the slender body of his companion as they forced their way steadily onwards.

Time ceased to have meaning. Time

became the gap between lifting one leg, thrusting it forward, and lifting the other, thrusting it forward, step after step, yard after yard. Sweat streamed down their faces, stinging their eyes, burning the sore skin where it had been rubbed raw by the harsh fabric of the suits. It was as if they walked through a clinging mass of glue. The water pressed against them, binding, mocking their every effort.

Progress was slow. Too slow.

Don halted, signalling Felling to make contact. The metallic clash of their helmets sounded startlingly loud.

'Felling. How much air do we carry?'

'About five hours. Why?'

'We've been moving for a long time now. Are you sure we're headed towards the shore?'

'No,' admitted Felling. 'I'm not sure. There's no way I can be sure.'

Don bit his lip as he glanced about the dim green water. 'Look. We could be walking in circles, or even further out to sea. We've got to orientate ourselves.'

'How?'

'Have you got all your binding twine?'

'Yes.'

'Good. We'll tie all the lengths together, make one long cord. I'll close my escape valve and inflate the suit. Tie the cord onto my foot, I'll drop the weights and rise to the surface, have a look around, then you can pull me down again.'

Rapidly they knotted the cord, and Don fastened it to his belt, then down past his boot. 'If I tug on the cord pull me down quick. Understand?'

'Yes. You going up now?'

Don grunted, closing the escape valve on the suit and unfastening the chest, and belt weights. Swiftly the suit bloated as the trapped air hissed from the tanks and built pressure within the suit. Slowly, like some monstrous balloon, he began to drift towards the surface.

Spray dashed against the face plate. Spray and a driving rain. It drummed on the metal of his helmet, dashed against the water sending up little gouts of drifting moisture. Irritably he wiped the front of his face plate and star, eagerly about him.

Sea. Sea and the drifting swell of rolling

waves. Tensely he twisted, jerking his body around in the water, straining to see in all directions. Something loomed low the horizon. Something looking like a distant cloud. Dark, indistinct, a black smudge against the grey of the cloud and the grey of the sea.

Land.

Land, and something else. Desperately he tugged the line and water bubbled around his face plate. Within minutes he stood swaying on the seabed while Felling replaced his weights. Cautiously he operated the escape valve, and like a punctured balloon the suit yielded to the pressure of the water surrounding him. Impatiently Felling made contact.

'Well?'

'Land lies in the way we're going, a long way off though.'

'Good. What made you come down so soon?'

'Patrol boats! They're as thick as fleas between us and the shore. The alarm must have gone out and they hope to catch us when we land.'

'If we land,' said Felling grimly.

'What do you mean?'

'How far did you think the shore was?'

'Hard to tell, ten miles perhaps, perhaps less. Why?'

'The air isn't going to last,' muttered Felling. 'We only started with about five hours, and we've been using it fast.' He fell silent. 'What shall we do, Don?'

'Use the spare tanks, that's why I brought them along.'

'No. We have no tools to make the exchange, and in any case there would only be enough air for one of us to make the shore.'

'Let's get moving,' snapped Don. 'We've air for a while yet, and when it's gone, we'll surface and swim the rest of the way. Move now, Felling. No use sitting and worrying about it.'

Grimly they plunged through the water.

Air! Don couldn't stop thinking about it. Air, the very essence of life. Without it they would die horribly of suffocation, their lives depended on the gentle regular hiss from tanks fastened to the backs of their suits. Don knew now why escapes from the sea farms were so rare, without air, a man was held tighter then if he were chained.

He staggered, recovering at once and wincing from the pain of his torn hands. Felling stood behind him, still trailing the long cutting tool. Impatiently Don plunged ahead. The going was rougher now. The jagged rocks and hidden crevices making progress even more difficult and slow. Little specks began to dance before Don's eyes, and his lungs strained for air. Mechanically he adjusted the air valves, increasing the flow from the tanks and clearing his mind from the effects of oxygen starvation. He paused awhile, breathing deeply, then gesturing at Felling, thrust impatiently onwards.

His head ached, his legs felt numb and dead. His eyes burned, and his bare hands, white and shrivelled from contact with the cold water, could scarcely adjust the valves. As the depth of water above them slowly lessened it became necessary to regulate the passage of air through the suits. Grimly he forced his numb hands to spin the regulating wheels of the tiny valves.

Felling stumbled and fell, Don gripped him by the belt and forced the slender man to his feet. Their helmets rang hollowly as he made contact.

'What's the matter?'

'I can't go on,' gasped Felling. 'Leave me, I'm all in.'

'Nonsense,' snapped Don with forced cheerfulness. 'We're almost there, just keep trying man, you'll make it.'

'No. No, I'll never make it. Listen, Don. If you get to shore call a man named Brenner. Mike Brenner. Central City, video 3879. Remember that. Central City 3879. Tell him that you knew me. Tell him . . .'

Desperately Don adjusted the valves on Felling's suit sending a blast of pure air through the man's helmet. Felling moaned, and weakly straightened.

'Remember that, Don. Call him, he will help you.'

'I'll call him,' said Don grimly. 'We'll both call him. Now pull yourself together man. We're almost there.'

He strode onwards, two steps, three, then stopped. A cold relentless hand seemed to grasp his heart. A cold relentless hand tightening even as he stood desperately listening. Listening to the unnatural silence.

The hiss of air within his helmet had stopped.

Frantically he spun the valves, then turned and gripped Felling.

'Felling. Quick! Listen to me.'

'Yes?'

'My air's gone. Now listen. I'm going to lash my wrists and waist. I want you to cut the suit below the lashing around the waist and above the wrist cuffs. I'll surface and get rid of the rest of the suit. Felling! Can you understand me?'

'Yes. How are you going to get rid of the helmet?'

'Cut the suit away after I've surfaced. I'll do the same for you. Now hurry!'

Quickly he tied lengths of the weighted twine about each wrist and around his waist above the belt weights. He tugged at the cord, ignoring the pain from the too tight lashings.

Felling followed his example, working clumsily with his numb hands.

With the razor edge of the cutting tool, Don slit the tough fabric of the suit, cutting around each wrist, then around his waist. Hastily, before the water could force itself past the lashings, he did the same for Felling. Gripping his cutter, he dropped the weights from his chest, then kicked himself free of the lower portion of the severed suit.

Rapidly he shot towards the surface.

He was gasping for air, fighting for it, gulping and feeling the terrible sickness as he strove for life itself. Water boiled around him as his helmet broke the surface, and he stared about with flame shot vision. He had no time to free himself of the rest of the suit. He had to breathe, and he had to breathe now!

Desperately he smashed his hand against the face plate of his helmet, again, again. The thick glass numbed his hand, sending little spurts of blood oozing from his fingertips, but the face plate remained intact.

Felling broke the surface near to him,

bobbing on the heaving water, Don grabbed at him, twisted his helmet, forcing Felling to turn away from him. The hard metal of the air tanks glistened in the water, and Don smashed the face plate of his helmet against the glistening metal.

Glass sprayed into his face, cutting and scratching his sweat stained skin. Water streamed through the splintered hole, water and life-giving air. Gratefully Don filled his lungs, savouring the salt tang of the moist air as he had never savoured anything before in his entire life.

Deliberately he smashed his helmet against Felling's face plate, and for a while they rested in the heaving water, helpless to do anything but breathe.

'What now?' gasped Felling.

'Get rid of these suits,' grunted Don, He drew a deep breath, ducked beneath the water, and with the cutter slashed at the lashings and the fabric of the suit.

Felling wriggled, disappeared for a moment. When he surfaced, he was free of the hampering bulk of helmet and air tanks.

Rapidly Don passed him the tool, and shed his suit in turn.

'Where is the shore,' gasped Felling. He looked sickly at Don, his pale face strained and blue with cold and exhaustion.

'There, see it? Like a low cloud.' Don frowned. 'It's further than what I thought, but the patrol boats have gone, that's one good thing.' He grinned at his companion. 'Think that you can make it?'

'No.' Felling coughed as a wave splashed into his face. 'I was never much of a swimmer, and I feel sick.'

'Bear up,' snapped Don. 'I'll help you, come on now, we'll swim together. Ready?'

'Ready,' whispered Felling. Together, side by side, they began to move slowly through the heaving waters.

It grew dark. Little stars shone in the sky, and a wind blew cold and wet from the restless ocean. Don swam with a mechanical regularity, his muscles numb and heavy, his heart thudding with exhaustion, his eyes burning with salt from the waves washing over his face.

Felling seemed a dead weight, his face strained and pale, livid in the soft starlight, his eyes like little pieces of brown glass.

'Goodbye, Don,' he said suddenly. 'You'll never make it carrying me. Remember what I told you.' He kicked, tore free of Don's supporting arm, and within seconds was gone.

'Felling!' croaked Don. 'Felling, come back here!'

Silence and the gentle slap of waves.

'Felling!'

No answer.

'Felling where are you?'

The wind blew cold and wet, sending the sea dashing in little waves and a mist of spray. The stars shone, clear and distant in the deep blue of the sky.

Tiredly Don headed for the shore.

9

The farm

Sand, and rain, and the lash of a bitingly cold wind. Don groaned, his limbs still automatically moving in swimming motions. He clenched his hands, feeling the harsh rub of gritty sand, and shivered as the rain-loaded winds lashed at his almost naked body.

Wearily he raised his head and stared about him, half remembering his last few minutes in the hungry sea. There had been waves, waves which had picked him up and thrown him hard against the rock and sand of a beach. He had crawled weakly away from the surf that had reached for him with salty wet fingers, crawled, and then collapsed with utter exhaustion. Now, beneath the spur of the chilly wind, he looked about him.

He rested on the slope of a sheltered cove. Low cliffs reared above him, their pale faces white in the glimmering starlight. The sea twinkled and muttered behind him, and he shuddered, remembering Felling. Numbly he climbed to his feet, biting his lips against the searing agony of returning sensation. For a while he stamped and moved in little jerks, slapping warmth into frozen flesh and movement into his sluggish circulation.

What could he do now?

Felling had given him a name, and a number to call. A video number at Central City, but first must come clothes, food, warmth, transportation to Central City, money for the video call, a dozen things, and he was frozen, almost naked and without the slightest idea of where he was.

The cliffs were of chalk, not high, but steep enough to make progress difficult. He left red stains as he climbed, blood from his lacerated hands and feet, but he was too cold to feel the pain. Grass replaced the chalk. Thin stringy grass, reed-like and sparse, growing with stubborn defiance on the sand at the edge of the cliffs. A bird rose with a whirr of wings as he stumbled over the low dunes, and a gull screamed in sleepy irritation.

It was dark, and cold, and the damp wind hissed between the dim shapes of twisted shrubs and rolling dunes. Sand lashed at him, the fine grains carried on the wind and scouring tender flesh with little stinging whips. Grimly he forced dead feet to carry him through the enveloping night, stumbling, staggering, half delirious with pain and exhaustion.

Slowly the moon rose above the murmuring sea.

A huddle of low buildings lay at the edge of a narrow road, lightless, seemingly deserted, the outbuildings of a farm. Don paused, restraining an impulse to hammer on the door and beg for help. Instead he crept cautiously up to the back of a house, and grinned a little as he saw the empty ghosts of clothing strung on a line. A dog barked, barked again with sudden swift urgency. A window banged, and a man's voice, tired and irritable, sounded hollowly in the yard.

'Digger. What is it boy? What is it?'

Don froze, pressing his body deep into

a patch of shade. The dog barked again, lunging with a clash of metal against the restraining chain around his throat. The man muttered something, half leaning out of the window and throwing the beam of a torch around the yard.

'Silence, Digger. Be quiet!'

The dog barked again, rattling his chain in a frenzy of noise. The window banged, lights streamed from the opened back door, and Don cursed the misery that had prevented him from leaving the farm.

Light bobbed over the yard. The man, a wrinkled elderly rustic, threw the brilliant beam into every dark corner, traversing the silent barns, the chicken roost, the dim shapes of farming machinery. The light swung, steadied, and Don could hear the sharp hiss of indrawn breath.

'All right. I see you. Come out of there.'

Don bit his lips and stumbled forward, he squinted, trying to shield his eyes from the blinding light.

'Who are you? What are you doing here?'

'Help me,' gasped Don. 'I've swum ashore, a long way. I was in a boat, it capsized, my friend was drowned.'

He paused, letting his appearance speak for itself. The man hesitated. In the silence the barking of the dog sounded strangely loud.

'Shut up, Digger!' snapped the man irritably. 'I've found him, go back to sleep now.'

He squinted at Don, then abruptly gestured towards the open door. 'Get inside.'

Don nodded, half fell through the open door, then, as the warmth of the room hit him, fell in a semi-daze. Numbly he lay on the brick floor, still conscious, still able to think and to reason, but unable to move. His body, overtaxed to the point of utter exhaustion, refused to obey his mental commands, and with a sudden quick relief from the necessity of further struggle, he lapsed into a stupor.

Something stung his lips. Something hot and burning trickled down his throat, he coughed, gasped, coughed again, the raw taste of alcohol sharp in his mouth.

He felt the rim of a glass held against his lips.

'Drink up,' ordered a voice. 'Slowly now.'

Obediently he sipped the brandy, and from his stomach a fiery warmth spread and drove the numb coldness from his aching bones. He shuddered, forced open his eyes, and stared at a wrinkled, seamed face, the colour of the soil its owner had tended for so long.

'Thanks,' he gasped. 'Thanks a lot.'

'Feel better now?' The old man sat back on his heels and looked at Don with little bright eyes. 'You look all in. Where are you from?'

'I told you. I was out in a boat, it collapsed, my friend was drowned, and I had to swim ashore.'

'So you told me.' The old man nodded. 'My name is Renfrew, Jarl Renfrew. I'm a tenant farmer, leasing the land from the government. Are you in trouble?'

Don blinked at the sudden question.

'Yes,' he admitted. 'Are you going to turn me in?'

'Maybe,' said the old man, 'and then

again, maybe not. Murder?'

'No. Self defence, but that isn't important. I broke my contract.'

'You on a sea farm?'

'I was.' Don stared at the old man's shrewd little eyes. 'What are you going to do?'

'There's no hurry,' cackled Jarl. 'I've no love for the sea farms. Don't seem natural somehow, growing stuff under the water. How can it be a farm without animals?'

'Are you going to help me?'

'Depends,' snapped the old man. 'What do you want?'

'Clothes, food, a night's rest.'

'What'll you do if I give them to you?'

'Do? What can I do?'

'We'll talk about it in the morning.' The old man glanced at Don and his little eyes glittered. 'You strong?'

'As strong as most. Why?'

'Nothing.' The old man cackled again. 'I can fix you up for the night, you can bed down on the floor, next to the fire. There's bread and cheese, that'll do for food. We'll see about clothes in the morning.' He stood up, and Don could see the soft light of the fire reflect off his little eyes.

'Goodnight, son.'

'Goodnight.'

Don sighed, forced himself to eat a little of the food, then stretched out before the fire. Sleep came almost at once, a strange sleep, one in which he relieved again the events of the past few hours. Once he started awake, and caught a glimpse of the old man peering down at him, then darkness overwhelmed him, the deep soothing healing balm of sleep.

It was light when he awoke, and the old man pottered over the fire, stirring a blackened pot. Don lay quietly for a while watching him, then yawned and sat up.

'Good morning, son. Better now?'

'Yes thanks,' said Don. He rose, and winced at the pain from his torn feet. The old man jerked his head towards the door.

'Pump in the yard, better wash up before breakfast.'

The water was discoloured, brackish,

and as cold as the arctic. Don splashed his head, washed the dirt and blood off hands and feet, then finished by pumping water all over his bare torso. A strip of rough sacking hung on the pump, and with this crude towel, Don rubbed his skin until it glowed.

Breakfast consisted of a grey porridge, black bread, and steaming herbal tea. The food was rough, almost uneatable, and had a stale odour. The old man gulped his plate empty, tore at the bread with blackened snags of teeth, then sat sipping the pale green liquid in his chipped cup, as he stared at Don.

'There's clothes,' he grunted, jerking his head towards a shapeless bundle. 'They should fit you. When you've dressed, we'll get to work.'

'Work?'

'Yes. Farm work. I can use you here, it's getting too much for an old man.'

'I can't stay here,' protested Don.

'No?' The old man grinned, showing his ugly teeth. 'Perhaps you'd rather go back to the sea farm?'

'No.'

'Then you'll work here.' Jarl gulped the last of his tea. 'If you don't, you may find that I can get nasty, very nasty.'

'Look, old man,' snapped Don. 'You've helped me, and I'm grateful, but I can't stay here for long. I owe you something, I'll admit it, and I'll help you all I can, but after that I must get on my way.'

'Of course you must,' soothed the old man. 'All I want is a little help. You don't know how hard it is to run a farm nowadays. No labour, no machines, no fertilizer. If you'll just give me a hand until the new crops are in, that's all I ask. Not much to do for a poor old man who's saved your life is it?'

'No,' admitted Don. He glanced at the old man with sudden suspicion. 'Let's look at the farm.'

The clothes were old, patched, and fitted where they touched. Don wondered who looked the worse, he or the old man, then grinned as he remembered how he had been dressed. At least, now he was covered.

Together they wandered over the farm,

144

and as they went, Don's suspicions grew into a certainly.

The old man was mad!

The barns were rotting ruins. The hen roost empty. The yard a clutter of broken and useless farm machinery. Aside from themselves and the dog, the farm was devoid of life. The agricultural ground didn't exist. Where it once may have been, rose the slender towers of wind shafts, their propellers spinning in the sea breeze, their legs straddling a waste of salty marsh. Don looked questioningly at the old man.

'Where's the farm?'

'Where?' Jarl spun, his brown wrinkled features working angrily. 'Where do you think? There of course, can't you see?'

'I see the wind shafts, some useless sea marsh, and wind blown sand. Where are your crops? Where are your fields?' Don was deliberately cruel.

The old man stared for a long moment, then his round shoulders slumped, and tiredly he turned away towards the house.

'So it was a dream?' he muttered. 'I

145

should have known it, but I wouldn't see.' He paused and wiped a trembling hand across his eyes. 'I had a farm here once, a good farm. Then they built the wind shafts, then they let the marsh regain the ground I had driven it from years ago. Now there's nothing left. Nothing.'

'Why do you stay?' whispered Don. 'Why not go to one of the government farms? They could use a man like you.'

'No!' The old man glared his anger. 'No, I'll never leave here. My son died here. My wife. My life is here, why should I move?'

'You'll starve here. What can you eat aside from scrapings and filth? What if you fall ill, have an accident? Who could help you then?'

'You will.' The high velocity pistol glittered in the old man's hand, the tiny bore of the muzzle centred directly on Don's stomach. Jarl laughed.

'You're not the first man to have come here. There have been others, they lie buried beneath the stones of the yard. One of them had this pistol, he died when he tried to use it. You will stay here, and together we will work this farm. The soil is still good, some of it anyway, and there are seeds in the barn. The machinery is broken, and I haven't got any horses, but you're strong enough to pull a plough. You'll work, or you'll die. Well?'

'You're insane!' snapped Don. 'You don't know what you're doing.'

'Oh yes I do,' sniggered the old man. He gestured with the gun. 'Come on now, work! Get tools from the barn, till the soil, plant the seeds! Work! Work! This farm will live again!'

A white froth rimmed the slack mouth and the little eyes glared with insane energy. The pistol trembled in his hand, little splinters of light glittering from the polished metal.

Don sighed, and sharpened the focus of his mind.

'Put down the gun,' he said gently.

'No!' The old man staggered a little, rubbing at his forehead.

'Put down the gun!' Don strode deliberately forward, and snatched the weapon. For a moment he stared at the

147

old man, then his eyes softened, and he walked away. Behind him came an animal-like cry.

'Wait!'

Don continued walking, and the cries died in the distance

10

Refuge

The smoke coiled towards a leaden sky, a thick streamer of greasy black, spreading and widening as it was torn and distorted by the wind. A little knot of men stood and stared solemnly at a heap of smouldering ash, their faces heavy and strained, each busy with his own thoughts. They bore weapons these men, crude weapons, clubs, pronged handles, a shotgun or two, and one carried a bright new high velocity rifle.

A few women stood among the men. Women with tear-stained faces and yet with stern expressions. They glanced at each other, then at their men, and each one had the stamp of shame. A man moved into the silent circle, and stared at the ruin that had once been a house.

'Accident?' asked Don.

He looked tired, worn with constant

cautious travel, strained with the ever present need to guard against the roving patrols, the hovering heliocops, the invisible threads of an efficient search system. He had changed his clothes and money jingled in his pocket. His feet were sore, but the gun in his pocket still had its new polish, the mere threat had been enough. Criminals are mostly born, but many an honest man has turned technical criminal. Hunger, and the spur of desperation served to crush inborn dislike of the use of force.

And Don had been desperate.

He repeated his question, glancing at a middle-aged man to his left. 'Accident?'

'No,' grunted the man. 'Mutants.' He stared at Don. 'You're a stranger here aren't you? Where are you from?'

'Down the coast.' Don tried not to shudder as he stared at the smoking ruins. 'Headed for the city, I hear that there's plenty of work there.'

'Is there?' The man spat towards the fire. 'I wouldn't know.'

A woman on the edge of the crowd began to scream in an hysterical outburst caused by revulsion of a deed done too well. The man stared at her, then spat again in the fire

'Isn't that just like a woman? Now they'll be blaming the men for burning the mutant, and they were the ones who kept nagging about it to start with.'

'How many?' Don forced himself to remain cool.

'Only the one, but the mother fought to the last, we had to burn them both.'

'And the father?'

'He died early.'

'I see.' Don fell silent, trying not to show his emotion The man at his side grunted again, he seemed to welcome conversation.

'I can't see any sense in it myself,' he grumbled. 'We've had freaks before. There's always been freaks. It shouldn't be necessary to burn them, and that's all the mutants are, freaks.'

'What do the women think about it?'

'The women!' Scorn echoed in the man's heavy tones. 'I'd rather be at the mercy of a tiger than of a woman. They're insane. First they scream about safeguarding the purity of the race, then they

151

kept on at the men to destroy the mutant. Finally they torched the place and made us join them. I can't understand it. The mother was a normal woman, it's only natural she should try and protect her child, but to see those women tear at her . . . ' The man shuddered and clenched his big hands.

'It's fear,' explained Don. 'Fear that they, too, may give birth to a mutant child. The fear overwhelms them, destroys their sense of proportion, they think that by killing the mutant they can kill their own fear. They can't of course.'

'Sounds sensible,' said the man. He moved towards a ramshackle car. 'You want a lift to the city?'

'Thank you,' said Don. He slipped into the proffered seat. 'How far to go?'

'I'll drop you off a few miles, kilometres I mean, from the outskirts.' The man grinned. 'I still can't seem to get hold of this metric system. Miles seems more natural somehow.' He slipped in the clutch and the turbine whined with a grating inefficiency.

'Much of that going on?' Don gestured

at the thin column of smoke vanishing behind them.

'Too much.' The man's big hands knotted around the steering wheel. He stared grimly before him. 'I don't like it, it reminds me too much of a flock of turkeys, they will kill a strange bird you know. Humans shouldn't be like that. If I had a child . . . ' His voice trailed into silence.

'Sterile?' asked Don.

'My wife, but I won't divorce her, and she certainly won't divorce me.' The man grinned. 'I'm lucky in a way, living out here we don't get all the hysteria they get in the cities. Women are the boss, but somehow they don't seem to remember it so much out here.' His face darkened. 'At least, not always.'

For a while they rode in silence. It grew dark, and the lowering clouds spilled a fine mist of rain. The car shuddered to a halt and the man gestured to a road leading into the distance.

'I swing off here. The city lies that way, you should make it about nightfall. Luck.'

The car whined off as Don lifted an

arm in farewell salute. Grimly he plunged on through the strengthening rain.

It was late when finally he stumbled into a public video booth. The lights of the city stretched away from him into the distance, casting a cold yellow glare over the deserted streets glistening in the rain. Numbly he fed coins into the machine and waited for the screen to clear.

'Your number?'

'3879.'

'One moment please.'

The screen swirled with ever-changing colour, then settled. A man's thin face stared at Don.

'Yes?'

'I want to speak to Brenner. Mike Brenner.'

'Nobody here by that name. You must have the wrong number.'

'That is Central City 3879 isn't it?'

'Yes.'

'Then get me Brenner. This is urgent.'

'Who's calling?'

Don paused. The man wouldn't know him, but he would know Felling. Explanations could come later.

'Tell him, Felling. Got that? Felling.'

'Wait.'

The video hummed, the screen blank and mirroring a plainly papered wall. The thin man returned,

'Where are you?'

'I'm not sure. On the edge of the city, public video booth, 845. Does that help any?'

'A little. Wait there, we'll pick you up. Right?'

'Right.'

The screen went dead.

Impatiently Don waited in the chill wind, hunching his shoulders against the driving rain. He stood in a shallow alcove several feet from the video booth, and watched the deserted avenue for signs of guards. A car drew up with a soft whine from its turbine.

'Felling?'

'Yes.'

'Get in.'

The car was empty but for the driver. Gratefully Don sank into the soft cushions, and felt the smooth acceleration pressure from the powerful turbine. They drove in silence, he wheels humming as they threw up a cloud of spray. The journey was short.

A man jerked open the door of the car and curtly gestured for Don to follow him into a narrow alley. A door opened to a series of raps, and light glared from brilliant fluorescents. Warmth coiled about him, warmth and the soft murmur of distant voices.

A man sat at a table and stared at him. A slight, almost boyish man, with soft brown hair, soft brown eyes, and a pale white skin. He smiled with a gleaming flash of teeth, and moved his hand in a curious gesture. A gun glimmered in one pale white hand.

'All right, you,' he said softly. 'Where's Felling?'

'Dead.' Don stared about him, and deliberately sat down. He felt tired, the warmth and the close air affected him after his long walk. Water squelched in his shoes, and faint steam arose from his soaking jacket.

'Explain.'

'We worked at the sea farm together,

you know about that?'

'Yes.'

'The overseer, a man named Carson, tried to get me to accuse Felling of being a Green. I had a fight with another worker, a man named Ed. I killed him. I thought it was about time that Felling and I made a break for it. We had to surface, ran out of air for the suits. Felling had a feeling that he wouldn't make it, he told me to call you if he didn't, said that you'd help me.' Don shrugged.

'We had to swim a long way. I did my best to support him, but the cold and the journey proved too much for him. He kicked free, and sank.'

'You mean he gave himself up for you?'

'Yes.'

The slight man narrowed his eyes and glanced at someone behind Don.

'Is he telling the truth?'

'As far as I can make out, yes.'

'I see. What's your name?'

'Burgarde. Don Burgarde.'

There was a sibilant hiss of indrawn breath from the man behind Don.

'That explains it. That . . . '

'Hold it!' The slight man stared at Don. 'Did Felling talk to you? Get really close, I mean?'

'Yes.'

'What did he say?'

Don smiled and stared at the pale faced man. 'I don't like guns pointed at me,' he said mildly, then concentrated his mind. Nothing happened. He frowned, sending his mental energy in sharp focus. The slight man shook his head, looked puzzled, then smiled.

'It doesn't work,' he said gently. He lowered the gun and relaxed. 'Now we are getting somewhere. What did Felling talk to you about?'

'Who are you?'

'Brenner. Felling was my brother.' Brenner smiled. 'Naturally he used a different name at the sea farm.' He leaned forward seriously. 'What did he talk to you about?'

'The Greens, and other things.'

'Yes?'

'He said that I was a mutant.'

'Are you?'

Don shrugged. 'I don't know. It seems I

have the power to disturb the thought processes of others. That is,' he corrected, 'I had. It doesn't seem to work on you.'

'It wouldn't,' said Brenner drily. 'Remember, I'm Felling's brother.'

Light suddenly dawned on Don. He sat up in his chair. 'Then . . . ?'

'Exactly. I'm mutant also, a successful one, and so are you.'

Don sat silent, thinking of a column of black greasy smoke. He shuddered, and felt someone's hand grip him reassuringly on the shoulder.

'I don't understand all this,' he muttered. 'How did I get into the sea farm? How is it that I didn't know what I was? Who are you, and what was Felling doing at the farm?'

'Steady,' said Brenner gently. 'You need rest, you've had a hard time.' He looked at the man standing behind Don's chair. 'Take him upstairs, get him some food, clothes, let him rest.' He grinned at Don. 'You can stop worrying now, we'll take care of everything.'

'Come on,' said the man Don hadn't yet seen. He stepped forward, and Don swallowed and tried not to vomit.

The man had a head three sizes too big for him. A great nodding ball of a head set on a pipestem neck and a child's body. His huge eyes were pale, lashless, and filled with an indescribable sadness. His little mouth pursed at Don's involuntary expression of horror, and his voice was low and almost bell-like.

'I understand,' he said gently. 'I too am a mutant. An unsuccessful one, a telepath.' He sighed. 'Shall we go?'

Don nodded. 'Sorry,' he apologised with real feeling 'I didn't know, it was the shock.' He paused helplessly.

The telepath smiled, his little mouth twisting repulsively. 'Never mind the apologies, remember that I can read your mind, I know what you feel.' He hesitated. 'My name is Vennor. If you want me, concentrate. I shall be able to pick up your thoughts.' He smiled again. 'Try to get used to my appearance, we will be much in each other's company.'

'Vennor will work with you to develop your latent ability,' explained Brenner. 'As one of us you will have much to do, and you won't be fully capable until you've had training.' He held out his hand. 'Goodnight now.'

'Goodnight.' Don released the boyish hand and turned to follow his new teacher.

They went through a narrow corridor, and as they went, the soft sound of voices grew louder. The telepath paused by a panel and turned to Don.

'I will leave you here. Go through this door, across the room, and up the flight of stairs opposite. Your room is the second on the right.'

Don nodded. 'And you?'

'I will see you after you have rested. Goodnight.'

'Goodnight,' said Don, and stepped through the open panel.

He frowned, then turned as if to go back, but the panel had closed, hidden in the decoration of the wall. He shrugged, and faced the room again. It seemed to be the annex of a gaming room. From a curtain-hung archway, came the click and rustle of cards, the metallic rattle as an ivory ball spun around a moving wheel, and the steady age-old drone of a croupier.

'Faites vos jeux. Rien n'a va plus.'

'Place your bets,' muttered Don wryly. 'No more play.' For a moment he hesitated by the thick curtains, then remembering his sodden clothing, headed for the stairs leading to his room. As he passed the curtains, they billowed and revealed two men emerged talking earnestly, and before he could stop, Don had bumped into them.

'Sorry,' he apologised. 'No damage, I hope?'

'No,' grunted one of the men. For a moment he and Don stared at each other, then Don smiled and continued on his way. The man stared after him.

'Anything wrong, Mr. Le Roy?'

'No,' said the man with muddy eyes. 'Nothing wrong.'

Hastily he left the building

11

World in Torment

The rain lashed against the high windows, streaming down the glass and distorting the twinkling lights of the city far below. From the concealed speaker an emotionless voice droned an uninterrupted stream of news items the murmuring voice blending with the faint hiss of the rain.

'Three new cases of mutant destruction reported within the past twenty-four hours. Green rioting at site of volcanic pit number seven. Food shortage in Eastern Zone blamed on mutated grain rust. Power rationing in Central Europe . . . '

Lyra sighed and switched off the speaker. A low buzzing came from the video set on her desk, and automatically she flipped the activating switch.

'Yes?'

'Dr Moray wishes to speak with you.'

'Connect him.'

The screen swirled and the sensitive features of the Director of Volcanic Power stared at the dark beauty of the secretary.

'Lyra?'

'Yes.'

'Use scrambler setting 259.'

Quickly she adjusted the vernier settings of the scrambler and the screen steadied into brilliant life.

'What is it?'

Moray sighed, and ran a hand through the thick mane of his snow-white hair. He looked worried, and Lyra saw him glance over his shoulder.

'If you think that we can be overheard,' she snapped, 'break contact.'

'No. With the scrambler and direct beam transmission we are safe enough.' Moray sighed again. 'I'm worried, Lyra.'

'What about?'

'Someone has been talking. Do you remember when you were here? We found something in the pit. Remember?'

'The coal? What about it?'

'The news has leaked out. Did you know of the Green demonstrations we've been having?'

'Yes.' Lyra frowned. 'Does the fact that you found coal mean so much?'

'Too much.' Moray wiped his glistening forehead. 'You wouldn't know just how important that discovery was, Coal is the most important mineral on Earth at this present time. There is nothing we can't do with it. Dyes, oils, medicines, food — a thousand things. If that seam were to be worked it would mean a constant supply of essentials for years to come.'

'Then why did you hide the discovery?'

'Don't you know?' Moray smiled tiredly and shook his head. 'Once the Matriarch had learned of the coal, she would have been forced to suspend operations on this pit. That coal would have been mined, fed to the factories, the project in this area would have been abandoned, the pit converted into a mine. This pit, Lyra,' he said with meaning. 'Pit number seven.'

'I see.' For a moment she stared at the flickering screen. 'Did you remember the name of the Matriarch's sister? Her married name, I mean?'

'Yes. Burgarde. Rex Burgarde. He was

an officer in the interceptor squadron.'

'I'd guessed as much, it fills in a gap.' She smiled at the worried face before her. 'What are you concerned about, Moray? The pit is sealed, it is only the word of one man against yours. Rush construction at full speed, haste is essential.'

'You mean?' Moray stared at her and suddenly he seemed very old.

'Yes, doctor.' Lyra smiled at him, then cut the connection. For a moment she leaned back in her chair, her slanted eyes closed, and little lines of fatigue clear against the faint bronze of her skin. Then she stirred and pressed concealed buttons beneath the wide desk.

Rapidly she attached the tiny instruments, and felt rather than heard the hidden surge of power.

'Yes?'

'Contact four three nine.'

'Contact four three nine. Proceed.'

'Cease all demonstrations at site of volcanic power pit number seven. Cut down all demonstrations at all volcanic power pits. Kill any mention of coal.'

'Yes?'

'Information on Burgarde. Don Burgarde.'

Silence, and the hidden surge of power.

'Escaped from sea farm. Present whereabouts unknown.'

'Watch. Guard if found.'

'Understood. Off?'

'Off.'

Power died, the tiny whispering voice died, and slowly she returned the instruments to their hiding place. A light flashed before her, and tiredly she rose and crossed the room.

Mary Beamish, Matriarch, stared at her from little piggish eyes, and petulantly pursed her thin mouth.

'You took your time answering, Lyra.'

'I came at once, madam. Your wishes?'

Irritably the old woman rustled some papers on the ornate desk before her. 'I just wanted to show you that in some things you aren't as clever as you like to think. What about these riots?'

'What about them, madam?'

'Getting out of hand, that's what they're doing. Have you heard the latest reports?'

'Some demonstrations at one of the power pits. Nothing to worry about.'

'No?' The Matriarch smiled with ugly mirth. 'Do you know who are the leaders of these Greens? No? I thought not. Well, I do.'

'Yes?'

'Remember those names I gave you and told you to have eliminated? You stopped me then, but this time I won't be stopped. Look at them! I tell you that those people are the Green leaders!'

'Surely not.' Lyra smiled a little as she stared at the old woman. 'The Greens are simply a few fanatics letting off steam, what harm could any of them do but shout?'

'Harm enough,' snapped the old woman. 'While they contented themselves with stupid meetings and local agitation, I agree they did little harm, but now they've gone further than that.' She paused, deliberately keeping her secretary in suspense.

'Well?'

'I have a secret report here from my own intelligence department,' she smiled, enjoying her triumph. 'Oh, yes, I have my own methods, I'm not content to dance to your tune, my girl.' She slapped the papers. 'For several months now there has been a constant and increasing theft of vital material.'

'There have always been thefts of vital material,' Lyra said tiredly. 'Workers will always help themselves to a little food. Others will steal metal and saleable items. We have known of it since the dawn of history, it's nothing new.'

'No? Then what about the theft of uranium, and other fissionable ores? What about the theft of large stocks of titanium alloy, radio equipment, concentrated food, a dozen different items? I'm not talking of petty pilfering, but wholesale theft. What about that?'

'Uranium?' Lyra lifted her eyebrows. 'From where? How comes it that there have been stocks of fissionable elements kept to steal?'

The Matriarch shifted uncomfortably in her chair. 'A precaution, nothing more. The government has retained some atomic weapons for use in an emergency, it is those that have been stolen.'

'I see.' Abruptly Lyra began to laugh. 'So you've lost your precious atom bombs, and there isn't a thing you dare do about it. If the people ever knew that the Matriarch condoned the retaining of atomic weapons, they would revolt, and you know it.'

'That isn't the point,' snapped the old woman. 'The bombs have gone, stolen by the Greens, and we've got to get them back. Get them back or render them harmless.' She banged her mannish hand hard onto the desk. 'Can't you see what this means, Lyra? With those bombs the Greens can deliver an ultimatum, and if we don't yield, they can destroy civilisation. You know as well as I that we can never survive another atomic war.'

'They won't start another war,' promised Lyra grimly. 'The Greens aren't fools. In some ways they are the most intelligent people on this planet. They know the effects of atomics too well to add to the destruction already done. You needn't worry about the lost bombs, probably they were stolen just to prevent their use.'

'Perhaps, but I'm taking my own precautions.'

'As you wish, and now what about the mutants?'

'The mutants?' The Matriarch stared her surprise. 'What about them?'

'They are still being destroyed, murdered by bigots and insane members of the population. Why don't you issue a decree granting every mutant amnesty, and forbidding the baby murders taking place at this moment? Issue a decree, and enforce it with the full power of the guards.'

'Those mutants!' The old woman gestured petulantly. 'Why you worry about them I don't know. What harm can they do? And what harm can the deaths of a few of them do? It is only natural that a mother should want a normal child. How can you expect any woman to rear a monster?'

'I can and do!' Lyra stared at the old woman, little spots of red glowing in the smooth bronze of her skin. 'Those babies are the innocent results of man's own inhumanity to man. You can't deny a thing by destroying it. Like it or not, those children are the future generations. How can we expect to continue the race when we kill fifty percent of our young?'

'We must keep the race pure,' snapped the old woman. 'Anyway, your figures are inaccurate.'

'Are they?' Lyra smiled tiredly and stared at the driven rain streaming down the windows. 'How do you know? How do you know how many births are unrecorded? How many women terminate their pregnancies? You can't know.'

'Neither can you.'

'Exactly? No, I agree, but recorded births of all groups come to less than one third of a comparable period prior to the atom war. Of these births, one half die before the age of three years. Of the remainder, one quarter never reach maturity. Add sterility. Add recessive mutations. Add murder, suicide, and undesirable hereditary factors such as haemophilia, and what have you left?'

'The race must be kept pure,' insisted

the old woman stubbornly.

'Which race? The human race? That is extinct, murdered by its own hand. Children born today are not human as those born prior to the atom war were human. Too much radioactivity has been scattered around for that. The very chromosomes of the race have altered, disrupted by the insane misuse of atomic power. How many are sterile? How many mutants can ever hope to breed true? What is the future of the people of the earth unless they are given every chance to regain their heritage, the heritage of a new world. For it is a new world. New peoples, new animals, new sources of power. You are of the old generation, the greedy generation, the insane era. You have no right to determine what world the new race will live in, you are capable only of humbly trying to undo your wrong.'

'Are you mad?' The Matriarch stared at her secretary in sudden doubt. 'How dare you talk to me this way? I am the Matriarch! I rule! I determine what is best for my people! How dare you!'

'I dare because I am of the new generation, I have to live in this world, I and my children. It is to me and those like me the world belongs, not to old women spitefully avenging themselves on long dead dreams.'

'Get out.'

'Yes. Yes, I'll go, but for your own sake and the sake of the world, think of what you do.'

'Go!'

Lyra sighed, looked at the old woman who seemed about to say something, then, as she appeared to change her mind, moved to the door.

'Will there be anything else, Madam?'

'No.'

'Goodnight, Madam.'

The Matriarch didn't bother to reply. She stood staring at the rain-wet windows, heavy lines engraved on her old features. She didn't seem to hear the soft closing of the door, but abruptly, with a sudden collapse of self control almost ludicrous in one so old and stern, she broke into a storm of weeping.

Blindly she fumbled her way to the

wide desk, slumping in the cushioned chair, and resting her head on her arms. It was very quiet, not even the thin drumming of the rain served to drown the harsh racking sobs, and the tears traced wet paths down the channels of her aged face.

For a long time she wept, the body-shaking sobs gradually easing as she managed to control her emotion. Finally she lifted her head, dabbing angrily at her eyes. Blindly she fumbled with the controls of a video.

'Yes, Madam?'

'Connect me with Le Roy.'

Silence as the operator sought for contact, then . . .

'I'm sorry, Madam. Le Roy is not within calling range. His whereabouts are at the moment unknown.'

'Send him to me as soon as you contact him.'

'Yes, Madam. Will that be all?'

'Yes. No, wait.' The Matriarch hesitated, her finger quivering on the controls. 'Contact Doctor Moray. Volcanic pit number seven.'

'Yes, Madam.'

The screen swirled, steadied into a brilliant flickering pattern framing the tousled hair and sensitive features of the old doctor. He frowned, his features registered a blend of surprise and apprehension.

'Yes, Madam.'

'You remember me, Moray?'

'Naturally. You are the Matriarch.'

'I don't mean that. Do you remember me a long time ago?'

Moray swallowed. 'Yes, Mary,' he said gently. 'I do.'

'John,' she said softly. 'John, I'm so miserable.'

'I understand.' He glanced over his shoulder. 'Set your scrambler on 365.'

Numbly she adjusted the setting on the video, then frowned at the clearing screen.

'Why did you do that?' she snapped tersely. 'Who would dare to intrude on the Matriarch?'

'Listen,' he said urgently. 'Who would do what doesn't matter now, but there's one thing I must know.'

'Yes?'

'Are you going to continue with the volcanic power project?'

'Why, yes. Is there any reason why I shouldn't?'

'No.' Moray licked his lips and absently smoothed his ruffled hair. 'You realise how important this is, don't you? You know that what we're doing means the salvation of civilisation, a continuous source of cheap power?'

'What's the matter with you, John? You sound like an old woman. I called you because I wanted cheering up. My secretary upset me, something that she said. Am I a hateful old woman, John?'

'Did she say that?'

'Not in as many words, but the feeling was there. Am I, John?'

'No, Mary. I wouldn't say that, but aren't you being just a little bit stubborn?'

'How do you mean?'

Moray shifted a little, looking startlingly like a guilty schoolboy. He glanced down at something beyond the range of the video transmitter.

'It's about the mutants, Mary. Don't

you think that you should sign an amnesty?'

'What good will that do?' she snapped. 'An amnesty for what? What crimes have they done which need forgiveness?'

He looked at her with a peculiar expression.

'The crime of being born,' he said gently. 'The crime of being alive.'

Irritably she switched off the screen.

12

Mental Awakening

'Try again,' said Vennor. 'This time concentrate on the electron flow in the wire.'

Don frowned, then deliberately relaxed, keening the fine edge of his mind. On a table before him a paper-thin wheel hung on jewelled bearings within a transparent vacuum flask. Tiny wires led from a motor no bigger than a thimble, connected both to the wheel and to a fine scaled ammeter.

Vennor threw a switch and the wheel spun soundlessly on its bearings. 'Now!' he said.

The wheel hesitated, jerked a little, then reluctantly reversed its direction. The needle on the ammeter flickered, then steadied, the wheel spinning with a sudden burst of energy in its original direction. Don sighed.

'I can't seem to control it,' he complained. 'I can inhibit the electron flow for a while, but no more than that. What is wrong, Vennor?'

The telepath pursed his lips and stared thoughtfully at the machine,

'It could be any one of a thousand things. We could be looking for the wrong answer, perhaps your talent isn't quite what we think.'

'Felling said that I was able to disturb the process of normal thought, break the trend, and cause the subject to forget what he was thinking about. It works. It worked on Ed, and on a farmer I met, but it doesn't work through metal and water, and it didn't work on Brenner.'

'It wouldn't,' agreed Vennor. 'A mutant doesn't have quite the same neural structure as that of an ordinary man. The cells of the brain are a little different, the neuron paths more flexible. When you tried to inhibit Brenner's thought patterns, he merely switched to a different set of neuron paths.'

Don sighed and stared at the little machine.

'Will I ever be able to control it as you think I should, Vennor?'

The telepath shrugged. 'Who knows? There are thousands of mutants in the world today who have not the slightest idea that they are anything but normal humans. They have latent talents, unsuspected, untrained. There are the men who have hunches, not realising that they are clairvoyant. There are lucky gamblers, who actually force the dice to fall as they wish, but who never think of themselves as other than just lucky. The women who have highly developed feelings of intuition, the people who seem to have the faculty of doing just the right thing at the right time. All mutants. All untrained, and all unsuspecting of what they really are.'

'I see.' Don looked thoughtfully at the grotesque figure beside him. 'What about you? How did you develop your telepathic powers?'

'I looked normal when born, babies always have heads larger in proportion to their bodies. It wasn't for some time that my parents noticed anything wrong, and by then I had developed the power of sensing emotion in those around me. My mother was shocked, disappointed, worried, but she was determined to protect me. I was the only child she could ever have.' Vennor stared grimly at the little machine on the table.

'She had forgotten the neighbours. Other women began to notice me, they began to talk, to whisper among themselves, soon the word 'mutant' was heard, and I could feel the intense hate directed towards me.'

'Then what happened?' Don couldn't stop remembering a thick greasy plume of black smoke.

'They came for me. The women, and their men. My mother defied them, my father also, it was useless. I was still very young at the time, not yet five, but I could feel the hate and fear flowing around me like a river of filth. I crawled from the house and hid among some rubbish. It was dark, and I was very small. They didn't find me.'

'What happened to your parents?'

'Dead, both of them. Shot and torn, murdered, the house burnt and everything they owned destroyed.' The telepath shuddered. 'I lay hidden for a long time, then someone else came to look at the ruins of the house. I could sense that they weren't as the others, and so I drew them to me. They were childless, middle aged, lonely. They looked after me for a long while. When they died, I came to the city, and here I am.'

'And here you are,' murmured Don. 'But where is here? What are we doing in a gambling club? Who and what is Brenner? What is this all about?'

'All in good time,' soothed the telepath. 'There are some things yet to be explained, but they will come later. Now let's get to work again.' He stared thoughtfully at Don.

'I cannot enter your mind without your permission. I can sense the surface thoughts, but you have a natural barrier to any deeper investigation. Tell me. Have you ever had a severe mental shock? Amnesia? Anything like that?'

'Why do you ask?'

'There seems to be a blockage, a point of strain. Can you think of what could have caused it?'

Don frowned, began to shake his head, then suddenly remembered.

'There's something, something I can't remember.' He paused, collecting his thoughts. 'I was on a monorail, I had just been informed that I had lost my job as a pilot on the local lines and was directed to labour on the sea farm. I met a man on the train, we ate together, talked for a while. The next thing I knew was that I awoke at a sea farm.'

He looked helplessly at the telepath.

'I thought that it must have been a dream,' he went on. 'I just can't remember what happened on the monorail, after meeting that man. The more I think about it, the more dreamlike it becomes. I must have tried to run, been caught, drugged, and sent to the farm, but the thing doesn't make sense. Why should they have drugged me?'

'Can you remember what the man looked like?'

'No. He was just an ordinary man. Why?'

'We have found the mental blockage I mentioned. At that period of your life, you suffered an intense mental shock. A normal man would not have been affected quite so much, they are more accustomed to shock and are able to continue without obvious ill effects, but your mind is different to that of a normal man.' Vennor frowned and began to pace the floor.

'An intense mental shock,' he muttered. 'What shock could have caused what amounts to a total amnesia? What could have been so unpleasant that you had to forget it to remain sane?'

'I don't know,' Don said helplessly. 'Is it important?'

'Very. Your mind has been injured, we must heal the injury before you are fully capable of developing your hidden talents.'

'But how can we do that?'

'Hypnosis. Recall. There are many ways.'

'Do you know them? Could you operate the techniques?'

'I could, but are you willing?'

'Yes.'

'Good.' Vennor nodded, then from a box assembled a machine composed of mirrors and various screens of varicoloured plastic. 'I shall help you, but in the meantime I want you to stare and concentrate on these moving colours. This is a kaleidoscopic hypnotic inducer. The colours will weave and flow in an ever-changing rhythm of colour. Concentrate on isolating one pattern. Concentrate. Concentrate.'

The machine sprang into sudden life. A writhing blend of flowing colour shifting, changing, altering in smooth and harmonious patterns.

Don stared at the flashing screen, beside him he could feel the telepath gently massaging the base of his neck. The slender fingers moved to his temples and as from a tremendous distance he heard a soft gentle voice whispering commands.

'Sleep now. Sleep. You are tired. So tired. Sleep. Sleep. Sleep . . .'

The voice faded to an immense distance, the swirling colour seemed to swell and engulf the entire room. Don felt himself sinking, sinking, sinking. The universe was full of colour. It surrounded him, penetrated him, swallowed his every sense and thought. It strained at him, pulling and drawing him into a scintillating void of harmonious ebbing light. Tiredly he yielded to the soft persuasion of sound and light.

He slept.

Voices swirled at him. A smooth purring voice, mocking, horrible in its quietly threatening tones.

'*It won't hurt, Don. It won't hurt at all.*'

Pain. Flashing searing pain, and the brusque tones of a different voice.

'*He's dead. Heart failure.*'

He's dead! He's dead! He's dead!

Don gasped, jerked his head, and abruptly awoke. He rested quietly for a moment, his face and neck damp with sweat. He stared at his quivering hands, then at the calm face of the telepath.

'What?' he gasped. 'What was it?'

'Your mental shock.' Vennor rose and switched off the machine. 'You'll be better now, you have remembered, and the memory will hold no terror for you.' He smiled. 'It was a shock, the worst shock you could have had. You believed that you had died, that you were dead. Naturally your memories were dim about that period, you found it impossible to adjust the fact that you were alive with the knowledge that you were dead. Your brain merely cut out that disturbing factor, and of course you couldn't remember just what happened after the episode on the monorail.'

'So someone tried to kill me,' muttered Don.

'So it would appear.' Vennor stared curiously at the young man. 'Have you any idea who would want to eliminate you?'

'That's what the man asked me,' Don said excitedly. 'He asked me why the Matriarch should want me dead and he asked whether I knew a woman named Lyra.'

'Lyra!' The telepath gripped Don's shoulder with weak hands. 'Did he ask about Lyra?'

'Yes, at least I think that was the name. Why?'

'Can you remember what the man looked like?'

'No, as far as I can remember he was just an ordinary man, nothing special about him that would make anyone remember him.'

'Can you remember if you have seen him since?'

'No,' snapped Don impatiently. 'I told you that I wouldn't know the man again if I saw him.' He frowned. 'Funny thing though, I did see someone very much like him, but it must have been coincidence.'

'You saw someone. Where?'

'Here, last night when I crossed the foyer to reach this room. Two men came out of the gaming room. I bumped into one of them, and now I come to think of it, he did give me a strange look.' He laughed and shrugged. 'Probably my imagination.'

'But he saw you?'

'He couldn't help but see me. I told you, I bumped into him.'

'Did you speak at all?'

'Just apologised, said that I was sorry. Why? Is it important?'

'It could be,' said the telepath grimly. 'Very important.' He hesitated, glancing at Don. 'Wait here, I must see Brenner about this.'

Within seconds he was gone. Don smiled, and resumed his mental exercises. The little wheel spun, reversed, spun again. Grimly Don forced himself to concentrate the invisible currents from his mind, trying to feel the surging flow of electrons coursing through the delicate wires. He sighed, and settled back in his chair, eyes blank and unfocussed.

It was useless.

A little control seemed possible. A momentary alteration of the normal course of things, but true control eluded him. He could interfere, he could not command. Tiredly he stared at the little wheel, then abruptly switched off the power from the tiny motor.

Sitting, mind unfocussed, eyes staring at nothing in particular, he felt a faint stirring at the back of his mind, as if a tiny insect were crawling across the naked surface of his brain. He concentrated on it, trying to localise the irritation; suddenly he stared, his eyes widening in startled disbelief.

Within the vacuum flask the little wheel spun on its jewelled bearings.

Don frowned, then checked that the power circuits were open. The wheel spun, then gradually slowed to a halt, the finely machined surfaces sending little twinkles of light from the rotating edge.

Again he slumped in the chair, this time staring fixedly at the wheel. Desperately he concentrated, urging the tiny mechanism to move with the sheer force of will alone. The wheel trembled, turned a little, then stopped as he ceased his fixed concentration. Deliberately he let his mind relax, feeling again the stirring at the back of his brain.

It was a peculiar sensation. A tiny irritation, as if on the bared surface of his very brain. He concentrated on it, exaggerating the discomfort, and forcing himself to compress the feeling into a single pinpoint.

Within the flask the wheel commenced to spin.

Don smiled, and settled back in his chair. For a while he played with the wheel. Stopping it, reversing it, then spinning it so fast that it seemed to dissolve into a blur. Then he turned his attention to the overhead lights. They flickered, dimmed, then glared in sudden brilliance. Again he sought control of the surging electrons, feeling the prickling at the base of his skull as he activated his control.

Abruptly he became aware of voices.

They echoed like tiny whispers through his skull, tingling, sending little ripples of energy racing across the surface of his mind. For a moment he thought that he had beeome telepathic, then as he felt the hidden surge of power, realised that he was tapping a secret conversation conducted via some electronic device. Tensely he listened.

'Contact three eight seven.' It seemed to be a woman's voice, low, vibrant with power, and yet strangely devoid of emotion.

'Contact three eight seven. Proceed.'

'Speed. Critical period commencing. Locate Burgarde. Don Burgarde. Inform.'

'Burgarde here. Second class mutant. Undeveloped power.'

Don grinned as he focussed the surging voices. Things had altered since Vennor had left the room.

'Stand by. Action essential. Uranium theft discovered. Guard against Le Roy.'

'Understood. Guard yourselves. Burgarde?'

'Hold. Bring when requested. Off.'

'Off.'

The silent surge of power died. The voices died. Don sighed, and frowned with sudden suspicion. Footsteps whispered outside the room, and Vennor entered. His little childlike features seemed drawn and strained. He smiled weakly at Don, then almost fell into a chair.

'Shall we continue?'

'If you wish.' Don smiled, then activated the little wheel. It flashed and spun, shimmering in rapid changes of direction and reflecting the light of the overhead fluorescents in twinkling spears of brilliance.

The telepath sighed, and looked strangely at Don.

'So you have located your control. Good.'

'Does that make me a mutant of the first class?' Don watched the other as he spoke, then dimmed the lights, casting the room in darkness.

Vennor half rose from his chair, and suddenly Don felt the full force of the other's mind pressing against his brain. Savagely he fought the pressure, lashing out with his own mind, then abruptly caused the lights to flare with a harsh brilliance.

'Well?'

'What do you know?'

'Not enough. I've discovered my control. It appears to be a form of teleportation. I can force electrons to move as I wish, but that isn't important.'

'No? Then what is?'

'Who are you? The group, I mean. Why are we here? How is it that successful mutants hide away in a gambling house? What is this all about?'

'What do you know of the world, Don?' Vennor smiled tiredly and drew his thin hand across his eyes. 'Please. The lights.'

'Sorry.' Don cut the glare, dimming the

flaring light to a soft, warm glow. 'You were saying?'

'I asked you what you knew of the world. The real world, I mean, not the accepted one.'

'Food is short. Women have taken control of affairs from men. Mutants are destroyed when discovered, and the Greens are agitating for conservation of resources.'

'Correct, as far as it goes, but what lies beneath the surface, Don? Have you ever thought of that?'

'No. What does lie there?'

'A battle, Don. A struggle between two races. Homo Sapiens and Homo Superior. Normal mankind, and us.'

'But . . . ?'

'Yes, us, Don. You are not a normal man, you are of the new race, and our struggle is your struggle.' The telepath fell silent, staring at his child-like hands.

'I can't believe it,' whispered Don. 'I knew that there was trouble, of course — everyone knows that. Extremes are always bad, but things will level themselves off, they always have done. It only requires a little time.'

'No, Don. Not this time. Things cannot straighten themselves out, things have gone too far. Listen. You know that the birth rate is falling, that the majority of children born are mutants?'

'Yes.'

'Then isn't it obvious? Unless the mutants are left alone, to live, die, marry, bear their own children, then how can the new race get started? We must secure a breathing space, Don. We must have time to breed and grow. Not all mutants are capable of bearing children. Most are sterile, others cannot transmit their mutant characteristics. We need time. Time to find out by trial and error whether or not we can survive. The scales are weighted against us, Don, but left alone we have a chance.' Vennor pursed his lips.

'We are not being given that chance.'

'Then . . . ?'

'So we are at war. A secret undercover battle. Us against the others. The have-nots against the haves. It is the only way we can make war, but it is life and

196

death to us, Don. Life or death to the race of man.'

'I don't like it,' muttered Don. 'One war was enough, we, the Earth, cannot stand another.'

'I am not referring to an atomic war. We aren't fighting to destroy the planet, but to save it. Unless we can win a chance to be born and to grow without interference, then Earth will become a shambles. The race will die. The normal births will be fewer and fewer. Men, what there is left of them, will be too few to run industries, maintain communications. Like it or not, the mutants are the only ones capable of stemming this insane trend towards destruction.'

The telepath sighed again, looking at his hands.

'Not all of us can win. I am sterile, I shall never help to build the new world, but even I can see what must be.'

'Then why are we here? If there is war, then why not let us fight?'

'We *are* fighting. What else can we do? We must have more, and who would employ a mutant? Many of us, yourself for example, would be forced into menial labour. We operate a gambling house, it provides us with funds, and cover.'

Vennor rose, and twisted his slack mouth in a smile. 'The war is almost over, Don. Soon we shall know, one way or the other. Very soon.'

He smiled again, then left the room. Don sat, his mind in a turmoil of thoughts and questions. War! Strange hidden conflict. And he, without any chance to decide, found himself in the middle of it.

He shrugged, then concentrated on the little machine. Within the flask the wheel began to spin.

13

Discovery

The pit was finished, the gaping hole in the centre of the rolling plain deserted and empty of men. From the slender poles, brilliant light streamed down on the tremendous heaps of debris and abandoned machinery. Alone in the room at the top of the slender building, Doctor Moray stared down at the scarred earth, and nervously ran his slender fingers through the tangled mane of his hair.

The video hummed with quiet urgency, the screen flaring to life as he activated the circuits.

'Moray?'

'Yes.' The old man stared at the tight young face framed in the leather of a flying helmet.

'Are you ready for us?'

'Yes.'

'Good. Land in five minutes.'

The video hummed, then fell silent. Moray shuddered a little, then, wrapping himself in a thick coat, left the room. He walked briskly towards the edge of the pit, then stood staring into the starless sky.

Long minutes passed. Then something like an insect droned through the silent air. It came nearer, and a small heliocab hovered on spinning rotors. For a moment it seemed to hesitate, then, very slowly and gently, it settled on the dirt at the edge of the pit.

Two men jumped out of the machine, a third passed them a heavy metal container, and carefully they carried it towards the thin figure of the doctor.

'All ready for us?'

'Yes. One of the elevator platforms is still powered. Is that it?'

'It is.' The man who had called on the video called something into the cab of the helio, and it rose with a whirr of rotors.

'Let's get moving; we've a lot to do and not much time to do it in.'

Together the three men walked towards the elevator platform, and rapidly descended towards the bottom of the pit. For a while they rode in silence, then Moray nervously cleared his throat.

'Any trouble so far?'

The young pilot grinned, and eased the leather helmet where it chafed his neck.

'None. The Greens are keeping the Guard busy tonight. We've finished three other pits, this is the last in this section. The others were completed hours ago. Difference in time, you know, and we had to operate in the dark.'

He stared down into the thick blackness below them. 'Did you have any trouble setting the machinery?'

'None. The workers thought that it was concerned with the hydro-electric steam turbine system. They installed it strictly to plan.' The old man sighed. 'The cables have been connected and everything is ready to go. That is,' he corrected, 'as soon as you have done your part.'

'That won't take long,' promised the young man. He looked at the old doctor. 'What will you do afterwards?'

'Lyra wants me to join her at the Matriarch's palace. We can build the machinery, and build it well, but the human element still remains to be completed.'

'I see.' The young pilot bit his lips thoughtfully. 'I suppose that we can make do without the co-operation of the old girl, but it would make things a lot easier if she could be talked into doing as we ask.'

The platform ground to a halt and Moray snapped on a powerful torch. The humped bulk of machines loomed strangely menacing in the brilliant beam. 'Can you see?'

'I could do this with my eyes shut,' grinned the young man. He called to his partner. 'Ready now?'

'Ready.'

Together they bent over their container.

For almost an hour they worked in a strained silence. Then, with a grunt of relief, the young man straightened, and wiped the sweat from his glistening features.

'That's over!' He looked at the humped bulk of the machinery cluttering the floor of the pit. 'It won't take long.'

'When will it start working?' Moray peered at the machinery with anxious eyes.

'It's working now,' said the young man cheerfully. He jumped onto the platform, his companion close behind him. 'Let's get away from here.'

With a jerk the elevator commenced its long journey to the surface. Moray stared down into the blackness and licked his dry lips.

'Will it hurt us?'

'No. The potential takes time to build. It is building now, but is restrained by the radio trigger. When that is activated — *wham*! The whole potential lets go and the sparks will begin to fly. The only danger was in loading the machinery, and we took care of that.'

He looked curiously at the old doctor.

'Any regrets?'

'No. No regrets, but it seems as though things are happening so terribly fast. This was always to be sometime in the future, now I find that a dream has become reality, and in a way, I'm afraid.'

'That is natural,' explained the young

man quietly. 'It is human to be afraid of the unknown, but it is a misplaced fear. Somehow I feel that it's like going to a dentist, you hate the thought of going, you fear the moment of extraction, then when it is all over, you wonder why you were ever afraid.'

The platform jerked to a stop at the edge of the pit, and he stepped onto the slippery dirt surrounding the hole. The young pilot lifted a torch into the air, pressing the button in a rhythmic series of flashes. With a soft drone the heliocab dropped gently into view.

'Will you be all right here on your own?' The pilot stared at the old man. Moray nodded.

'I expect a relief soon, and then I'll leave to join Lyra. In the meantime I'll watch the pit.'

'Good. Are you armed?'

'Should I be?'

'Yes. If anyone tampers with those machines it could be serious. The Greens will soon be surrounding the pit, officially for a demonstration, but actually to prevent anyone entering the area. Here.'

Moray looked at the glittering thing in his hand.

'Take it. Use it if you have to. The Matriarch has her own men, and some of them as clever as we are.' He thrust forward the high velocity pistol, then climbed into the waiting heliocab.

'Goodbye.'

The old man raised an arm in farewell as the blast from the spinning rotors lashed at him. He stood watching the tiny craft until it vanished into the blackness, then with a wry grin at the object in his hand strode rapidly towards the slender building. He felt very cold and shivered a little as he walked.

The building was deserted, chilly, and with odd echoes sounding from the empty rooms. Hastily he climbed the stairs, gasping a little from the effort of the climb, but feeling warmer through the exertion. Light streamed from beneath the door of the top room, and gratefully he threw open the panel, letting a warm blast of air circulate about him. Automatically he threw off his coat, and strode across to the window commanding a view of the floodlit site.

Halfway there he stopped, feeling a cold chill creep around his heart. A hat lay on the low table next to the video screen. A brown hat, soft, with a wide ribbon and a little gaily coloured feather. A strange hat.

Slowly he turned.

A man smiled at him. A man of medium height, of medium weight and build. He had muddy eyes, glinting a little in the light from the overhead fluorescents. He held a thick stylo in his hand, and casually he gestured with the instrument.

'Hello, Moray. Surprised?'

The old man swallowed his fear, and smiled in return.

'Why, Le Roy! Why didn't you tell me that you were coming?'

'Should I have done?' The soft purring voice sounded mocking and full of secret mirth. 'I have been watching you, Moray. I've wanted to speak with you for a long time now.'

'Yes? What about?'

'About the power pit, and other things.'

'Such as?'

'Such as, who were those men you met tonight? What did you do down in the pit? I have a lot of questions, Moray. A terrible lot of questions.'

'Then why not ask them?' Moray smiled and deliberately sat down. 'I'm not afraid of you, Le Roy. I know you for what you are, a cheap killer. Did the Matriarch send you here?'

'No.'

'Then get out. I'm busy, and I don't like your company.'

Le Roy smiled, his muddy eyes enigmatic and strange beneath the shadow of his brows. Casually he lifted the stylo. 'For a man who isn't afraid, Moray, you talk too much.' Abruptly he sat up in his chair. 'Aren't you afraid? Don't you fear death? I could kill you, Moray, kill you now, and you know it. Kill you like this!'

His thumb tightened on the thick stylo in his hand. Something spat from the end, something small and sharp and discoloured at one end. It flew across the room, and thudded with a faint plop against the soft brown hat. Le Roy

207

smiled, and slowly rose from the chair.

'A poisoned dart, Moray. I have many more left in this little toy. I could put a dart anywhere you care to name, your ear, your eye, your cheek. Shall I demonstrate?'

The old man remained silent, staring down at the tiny dart.

'Shall we go now, Moray?' The purring tones hardened. 'Move!'

'Where are you going to take me?' Moray tried to prevent the quiver in his voice. 'Where are we going?'

'Down the pit.' Le Roy gestured with his weapon.

'Hurry now, or shall I go alone?'

'Wait.' The old man stepped across the room. 'My coat, it is cold outside, and I'm an old man.'

'Certainly.' Le Roy stood watching while the old director slipped on his coat. 'Now if you will give me the gun in your pocket . . . '

'What gun?'

'Give it to me!' With an angry movement the muddy-eyed man snatched the glistening weapon. He balanced it in the palm of his hand, then slipped the stylo into an inner pocket. 'You must think me a fool, doctor. I told you that I had been watching you for a long time. Now lead the way to the pit, and for your own sake don't try to be clever.'

Grimly the old doctor led the way through the building and outside into the floodlit area. He paused, looking over his shoulder at the other man.

'What are you going to do?'

'Go down the pit. I want to see what those men have done down there.'

'I see.' Moray hesitated. 'We shall need some lights; it is dark down there.'

'You have a torch, haven't you?'

'Yes, but . . .'

'It will do. Now hurry!'

Together they moved towards the edge of the pit.

Moray walked with numb resignation. He had been a fool! The young man had warned him, had even given him a pistol, and he had acted like a baby. It must be because he was growing old, but being old was no excuse for being stupid. He glanced at the slender poles supporting the glaring floodlights, then at the crude support for the one remaining elevator platform.

Absently he rubbed his slender hands through his mane of white hair.

From beyond the floodlit area, beyond the mounds of scattered débris, a faint murmur became rapidly louder. The screaming shouts of women, the deeper tones of men. Le Roy hesitated, then looked at Moray.

'What is that?'

'The Greens, they are demonstrating around the site. We get a lot of it.'

'Can they get in?'

Moray shrugged. 'Only if they break down the fence, so far they have never done that.' He smiled a little at the other's worried expression. 'What's the matter, Le Roy? Afraid that you can't get out?'

'I've a heliocab parked behind the administration building. I can escape by air.' He gestured with the glittering weapon in his hand. 'Now hurry, I'm getting tired of all this talk.'

They paused by the flimsy elevator platform. Moray stared thoughtfully into the night-filled pit.

'You know what's down there, don't you, Le Roy?'

'That's what I'm going to find out.'

'You may not like what you find. You may not like it at all. Have you ever seen the men who have been sent to the dead lands? Seen those who wandered among radioactivity? Have you ever seen those men, Le Roy?'

'Yes.'

'You still want to go down?'

Le Roy licked his thin lips as he stared down into the pit. 'Yes. You can't frighten me, Moray. You have only just left there, whatever it is you did down there cannot be too dangerous. Now do we go down together, or do I go alone?'

'Things aren't quite the same as when we left, Le Roy. Haven't you ever heard of time fuses? Delayed action? Do you still want to see what we did?'

'Yes.' Amusement tinged the heavy purring tones. 'You talk too much, Moray. Time fuse, you said? That is just what I thought. It would be amusing to disconnect it wouldn't it? Very amusing, but not for you.' He dropped all pretence of politeness, and jabbed the high velocity pistol into the pit of the old man's stomach.

'I'm not playing, Moray. I would very much like to kill you, perhaps I will anyway, but if you don't do what I ask, and do it quickly . . . ' He smiled gently as he toyed with the pistol. 'Have you ever seen a man shot with one of these? The bore is small as you know, but the muzzle velocity is high, very high indeed. The bullet makes a small hole going in, but when it comes out . . . ' He whistled. 'I could blow your arm off with a single shot. I could spread your intestines all over the edge of this hole. I could turn your head into a pulp of blood, brain, and bone. Don't tempt me, Moray. Don't tempt me.'

Silently the old doctor stepped onto the flimsy elevator platform. Desperately his eyes darted about for some means to prevent the killer from descending into the pit. He glanced up at the thin cable, then at the release control. Le Roy watched him, smiling sardonically.

'All ready, Moray?'

'Yes.' The old man licked his dry lips. 'Yes, I'm ready.'

'Good.' Le Roy stepped forward, eyes and gun centred on the trembling figure of the old man.

One step he took, a second, and then a third. He paused at the very edge of the platform, hesitated a moment, then stepped forward.

Abruptly Moray exploded into action. With frenzied desperation he threw himself against the other man, using the slight weight of his body to disturb Le Roy's balance. One great thrust he gave him, then sprang for the controls of the elevator. With a screaming whine from the overhead cables, the platform fell into the thick darkness.

Le Roy staggered, then, as his support fell away from beneath his feet, sprang desperately for the slippery dirt rimming the pit. For a moment he clung there, little avalanches streaming from his fingers, then slowly he pulled to firm ground.

He still held the gun.

The guard had slipped up his finger, and had stayed there eyen as the blood had oozed from beneath his nails with the effort of recovering his balance. Beside him, the thin cables of the platform whined as they spun from the drum and vanished into the depths.

Breathing hard with shock and reaction, Le Roy stared at them, then his mouth twisted and he raised the pistol.

Three shots, and the cable parted with a sound as of breaking string. Something crashed far below, crashed and screamed with hopeless despair.

14

Crisis

It was dark, and the gusty wind brought a warning of rain. Little knots of men and women stood on the street, talking among themselves and scowling at the terse orders of the women guards. An air of tension ran throughout the city. A feeling of something about to happen, and of the uncertainly of not knowing just what. The lights on the overhead standards painted everything with their harsh yellow glare, and little scraps of paper blew along the gutters, impelled by the wind.

The turbine hummed with smooth efficiency as they spun along the streets, and Don sat intently in the forward seat. He turned and spoke to the men in the back compartment.

'How do we get in the palace?'

'That has been arranged.' Brenner looked out of the side window, and tightened his lips. Next to him, the great head of the telepath nodded in rhythm to the motion of the car.

'Why am I to see the Matriarch?' Don stared at Brenner. 'Is it to do with Lyra?'

'Patience,' murmured the telepath. 'In a little while you'll know everything.'

Brenner muttered as he recognised faces on the street. 'The Greens are out in force tonight. I hope that they'll be able to control the reaction.'

'They will,' promised the grotesque figure at his side. 'We chose them for their stability.'

The whining of the turbine slowed, and gently the car slid to a halt. 'Shall I wait?' asked the driver.

'No. Return to the garage.' Brenner grinned at the man's pale face. 'Get some rest, take a drink, do anything, but stop worrying. You're not going to a funeral.'

'Aren't I?' said the man. Gently the car drew away.

Brenner grinned after it, then turned to his companion.

'Right. Now to get into the palace. Don, you follow us, and keep close.

Vennor, take the lead, you know what to do.'

The telepath nodded, then strode confidently forward.

It was easy.

It was too easy. As he crept after the others, Don wondered what he would do should they be challenged. From time to time, Vennor would halt, raise a hand in warning and stand as if carved from stone. A guard would pass, swinging her rifle, staring at shadows, somehow she never stared at the shadows concealing them, and Don wondered again at the telepath's weird ability.

Soon they were standing by a small door in the rear of the palace. Don caught a mutter of soft words, a repeated command, then the door swung open, and they were in the palace. A pale-faced woman stared at them, then, closing the door, led them to a small elevator. Brenner paused, catching hold of her sleeve.

'Is she alone?'

'She was.'

'Good. This elevator will take us

directly into her room?'

'Yes, it is her private one.' The woman hesitated, and Brenner smiled comfortingly. 'Stop worrying. It will be all over soon.'

'I know, but supposing something should go wrong?'

'It won't,' promised the slight man. 'That's why we are here.'

The doors of the elevator hissed before them, and Don felt the floor press against his feet as they were whisked upwards. Softly the doors hissed open. A murmur of voices echoed in their ears, and Brenner frowned.

'The girl told us that she was alone.'

'Wait!' The telepath stood, one hand lifted, his child's face twisted in concentration. 'Someone is with her. Listen.' Gently he drew aside an inner panel, and they stared into a luxurious room.

A woman sat behind a wide desk. A woman with soft black hair streaming to her narrow shoulders, oddly slanted eyes, and a skin of the palest bronze. She wore a uniform of black, high collared blouse, and slacks. A pattern of thin gold lines weaved in an intricate arabesque relieving the sombre colour of her garb. A wide band of gold was clasped to her left wrist, a band supporting an elaborate chronometer. Her long slender fingers were devoid of rings, and her well-shaped nails lacked varnish. She was smiling, but there was the hint of strain beneath her smile.

'You surprise me,' she said. 'Really, to even think such things as you've mentioned . . . '

'Please, Lyra, let us not pretend.' The speaker was hidden, but the soft purring tones made Don frown in sudden recollection.

'You have been clever,' continued the man, 'very clever. But for an accident I would never had suspected you, but once I did, the rest was easy.'

'Yes?' She was very calm.

'Yes. I met a man. I met him by sheer accident, at a building here in the city. Nothing in that, you say? Perhaps not, but, Lyra, the man I met was dead.'

'I didn't know that you believed in ghosts?'

'I don't, and it was that which started

me thinking. I had killed that man, and now here he was alive. Therefore he could not be dead, and yet I had killed him. Strange, isn't it?'

'If you say so.' Lyra glanced at her wrist. 'Now if you will excuse me I am due to see the Matriarch.'

She glanced at the hidden man, then sank slowly back into her seat. 'What are you doing?'

'Explaining a point of interest. Shall we continue?' The voice purred with heavy mocking. 'I should hate to spoil your beauty my dear.'

'Very well, what were you about to say?'

'Merely this. Only three people knew that I was assigned to kill that man. The Matriarch, you, and myself. The Matriarch would have no reason to save him, or if she did, she only had to tell me. I certainly would not on my own volition, that left you, Lyra. You saved that man's life.'

'Did I, Le Roy? Perhaps you missed for once in your life?'

'I never miss. No. I shot that man on a monorail. Before I could get to him a doctor examined him, at least, I thought that he was a doctor. Don Burgarde was pronounced dead. I was satisfied. And then I bump into him several weeks later, alive and well. What would you think, Lyra?'

'Nothing. I am not good at riddles.'

'I'll tell you what I thought. I thought that you had betrayed me, and then I asked why. Would you like to hear my answers?'

'If you wish.' She sounded very tired.

'You had warned someone that I would assassinate that man. That someone had followed me, was waiting until I struck. When I did, he stepped forward, administered an antidote, and pronounced the man dead. How was I to even guess what had happened?'

'Assuming that I had done all this, why should I have done so, and who would be willing to work for me?'

'Why, that's one question. Who? The Greens,' The soft voice chuckled with inner mirth. 'Yes, Lyra. You are the secret leader of the Greens. It was you who ordered the theft of the atom bombs, you who suppressed the discovery of coal at the volcanic power pit. You have been the hidden hand all along. No wonder the Matriarch couldn't understand how it was that the Greens eluded capture so often. You have been warning them of every trap and raid planned. You, Lyra. You traitor!'

'Am I, Le Roy?' She sounded amused and a little afraid. 'What if I have? What can you do about it now?'

'I can recapture the atomic materials stolen from the government arsenals. I know where they are. At the bottom of the volcanic power pits, hidden in the machinery. The Matriarch will be pleased to hear that.'

'How did you learn that?' Anxiety sharpened her tones. 'Who told you that?'

'A man named, Moray. He was a good man, he even tried to kill me, a pity he failed.'

'Was a good man?'

'Doctor Moray is dead.'

Silence filled the warm comfortable room. Beside him Don heard the hiss of indrawn breath. Surprisingly Lyra began to laugh.

'You fool, Le Roy! So you killed Moray, and think that you have done a clever thing. I tell you that you have dome nothing. Why did you think we hid the uranium at the bottom of the power pits? Hidden in the machinery you say? You fool! Not hidden within the machinery, but part of it! Atomic power piles, Le Roy. Atomic power. Now do you understand?'

'You . . . ' The man seemed to choke as he almost spat the word. 'Is that what you wanted? Ruination of the Earth? You she-devil!' He breathed loudly for a moment and when he spoke again the soft tones had lost their mockery.

'Atomics killed my father, made me what I am. You tell me now that atomic power is once more loose in the world. You shouldn't have told me that, Lyra. It was a silly thing to do. I am going to kill you for it. Do you understand? I'm going to kill you!'

'No,' said Don, and stepped into the room.

Le Roy turned, his face a mask of snarling anger. The weapon in his hand levelled, then jerked towards the ceiling, the sound of the shot mingling with a tiny shower of broken plaster.

Again he tried to level the weapon. Again it writhed in his gasp like a thing alive. Desperately he fought it, snarling like a maddened animal as the slender barrel refused to obey his commands.

Suddenly he threw it aside.

'You tried to kill me,' said Don evenly. 'I thought that you were a friend, and all the time you intended to kill me. That's all you're good for isn't it, Le Roy? Killing people I mean.'

'You . . . ' Abruptly Le Roy darted his hand to an inner pocket; when it reappeared it held a thick stylo. He grinned in wolfish amusement.

'Touch me and I kill the girl,' he warned. Don smiled.

'Try it,' he invited. 'See if you can.'

He stood with deceptive casualness just within the room, and stared at the muddy eyes of the man before him. The stylo twisted in the thick fingers. It rose, pointing at the ceiling, then wavered as Le Roy fought for control of the deadly weapon. Something spat from the tip, imbedding itself in the wall.

'You can't do it,' said Don. 'You haven't the power any more. You're finished, Le Roy. Finished for good.'

With a smooth motion he stepped forward, and snatched the stylo from lax fingers. Le Roy stared at him, a faint film of sweat glistening on his heavy features.

'What are you going to do with me?' he gasped.

'Do?' Don smiled. 'Watch.' He raised his fist, then deliberately struck the terrified man on the point of the jaw. The muddy eyes glazed, twisted upwards in their sockets, and like a man of straw, Le Roy slumped to the carpet.

Lyra stepped forward, 'Thank you,' she said sincerely. 'He was a dangerous man, I should have been more careful.' Tensely she glanced at Brenner and the telepath. 'Is everything ready outside?'

'Yes.'

'Good.' She glanced at Don and smiled. 'I'm glad you're one of us,' she murmured. 'Very glad.'

'What happens next?' asked Don, He stared about him. 'Who are you, I seem to remember seeing you somewhere before, on a video screen.' He snapped his fingers as memory returned. 'Of course! You are the Matriarch's secretary.'

'Yes, and you are her nephew. I want you to remember that. That is the reason I ordered you to be guarded from Le Roy.'

She glanced at the instrument on her wrist, and bit her lip in sudden doubt.

'What's wrong?' snapped Brenner. 'Is it time?'

'Yes, but if we could only persuade the Matriarch.' She stared at Don. 'It would be worth trying, and it may mean so much.'

'Is she important?' Brenner glanced at the secretary. 'Surely coming from you it would have the same effect.'

'No. Some effect I'll admit, and if necessary I'll do it, but it would be better coming from the elected head of the people. Her word has more power than mine, and she appeals to those who

matter the most, the women. She could appeal directly to the feminist element.'
Lyra stood thinking for a moment.

'It's worth the attempt. I'll call her, ask her to come up. We have nothing to lose anyway, and the critical period will need some degree of tolerance.'

She moved towards the table and spun the controls of the video, the screen flaring and swirling with colour. It steadied, and the calm features of a female operator stared at her from the screen.

'Yes, Madam?'

'Connect me with the Matriareh.'

'The Matriarch is not to be disturbed.'

'This is her secretary. Connect me at once!'

'Yes, Madam.'

The screen swirled and hummed, little flecks of fire darting across the fluorescent screen then . . .

'I'm sorry, Madam. The Matriarch does not answer.'

'Thank you.' Numbly Lyra switched off the video, her face hard and set.

'That does it,' snapped Brenner. 'We

have no more time to waste. Lyra, connect on full coverage and relay the message. Hurry girl!'

'Wait!' The telepath gestured for silence, his bulbous head tilted to one side. A frown puckered his distorted features, and his little mouth writhed in an agony of concentration.

'Someone is coming. I cannot read their thoughts, too much shielding metal between us. I cannot even tell if they are friendly or not.'

Silently Don stooped and picked up the high velocity pistol. Brenner drew a similar weapon from a hidden holster. Tensely they waited, the sudden drumming of rain against the windows sounding startlingly loud in the strained silence of the room.

Footsteps sounded. Heavy mannish footsteps. A door slowly opened, and a figure strode proudly into the room.

Mary Beamish, Matriarch, stared at the pointing muzzles of two deadly weapons. For a moment she stared as if unbelieving her eyes, then she gasped, and looked wildly about the room.

'Our apologies, Madam.' Lyra steped forward with smooth efficiency. 'We thought that you were some other.'

On the floor the slumped body of Le Roy groaned in returning consciousness.

15

Phoenix

'What is the meaning of this?' The Matriarch glared at the assembled men, at her secretary and briefly at the unconscious body on the floor. 'Who are you?'

'Who are what we are doesn't matter now,' snapped Brenner impatiently. He slipped his gun back into its secret holster. 'We must speak with you, Madam. There are things you must do, and do soon. Tell her, Lyra.'

'What do you mean? How dare you come here ordering me about? Do you know who I am?'

'Yes. You are the Matriarch,' Brenner said tiredly.

'Please!' Lyra stepped forward, and smiled at the old woman. 'Madam. We have reached a crisis in the affairs of the world. We would like your co-operation, but if necessary we can do without it.'

'Crisis?' The old eyes of the aging woman stared at the men and the gun in Don's hand. 'You mean revolt don't you?'

'No. There is no intention of overthrowing the government. All we want you to do is to broadcast an amnesty to all mutant life. We want you to do it now.'

'You and your mutants!' The Matriarch glared at her secretary. 'The way you worry about those things, anyone would think that you are one yourself.'

'I am,' said Lyra quietly.

'You're *what*?'

'I am a mutant. I have eidetic memory, and two hearts. I am a successful mutation. I managed to avoid discovery, and my doctors tell me I shall bear children. Does that surprise you?'

'A mutant! *Here!*' Abruptly the old woman strode across the room and flung open the inner door. 'Come in here, all of you.'

They followed her into the ornate room that was the centre of government. Brenner glanced at his watch and pursed his lips in angry indecision. Rain streamed down the high windows, and from the distant landing field, came the thin whistle of a jet liner taxiing for take off.

'Madam,' said Lyra quietly, 'tonight is the turning point in human affairs, and also non-human affairs. I am referring to the mutant, and non-mutant population of the Earth. We have been fighting a secret war. At any time you chose you could have stopped that war, all we asked was that you should grant all mutants an amnesty, recognize their right to be alive, and to be allowed to live as normal people. You refused to do that. Your predecessors refused. You have only yourselves to blame.'

'Blame for what?'

'For what we are about to do.' Lyra paused, and looked at Don. 'If I cannot persuade you, let someone closer to you than I speak. This could have been your child. This was your sister's child. You knew that of course, that is why you ordered his assassination. Why did you do that? Was it because your own child was a mutant?'

232

'How did you know that?' The old features twisted with emotion. 'Who told you that? It's a lie! He died. He died from . . .'

'He died because his mother had been exposed to unshielded radiation, and so had his father. This man is a mutant. Brenner here is a mutant. Need I tell you what the other man is?'

The Matriarch stared at the telepath's swollen head and shuddered. 'What do you want me to do?'

'Be kind. Broadcast an appeal on a world-wide radio coverage that all mutants born, all mutants alive should be treated with kindness and understanding. As a woman that shouldn't be hard to do. As a Matriarch, your words will be received with respect — respect and obedience. Will you do that?'

'I . . . ' She hesitated, glancing at the slender body of the secretary. 'Is that all you want me to do?'

'That is all.'

The old woman sighed, and turned to the video. Her fingers hesitated on the activating switch, and again she looked at Don.

The thick finger pressed the switch.

'Yes, Madam?'

'This is the Matriarch speaking. I wish to talk to the world. Report when the connections have been made.'

'Yes, Madam.'

The flaring screen died, and the soft hum of power from the video died amid the muted drumming of the rain.

'*No!*'

'What?' Startled, the Matriarch turned to face the open communicating door.

'No! You can't do that. You mustn't!' Le Roy, his muddy eyes burning with a desperate fear, staggered into the room. 'Wait. Madam, I beg of you not to do as they ask.'

'Le Roy. Get hold of yourself man. What harm can there be in broadcasting an appeal to the world?'

'Death. The death of all human life.' He staggered, snatching at the edge of the door for support. 'Ask them what they did with the stolen atomics! Ask them what they intend with the volcanic power pits! Ask them what they really intend to do with the human race! Ask them!'

Brenner muttered a curse and stepped close to the reeling man, his pistol slipping from its hidden holster. Don stepped forward, his own weapon raised.

'Hold it!' He smiled at the delicate features of the secretary. 'I too am interested in hearing the answers. Well?'

'We mean no harm, Don. Believe me when I say that.' She paused, staring at the instrument on her wrist. 'It is true that the stolen uranium has been used to build atomic power piles at the bottoms of the power pits. The fantasy of a self-circulating water system was a blind to enable them to be built. Any good physicist would have shown the fallacy of that theory. The network of cables interlacing the world will carry power, that part is true, but it will be power derived from the atom, not the clumsy hydro-elecric steam turbine system. In that we have not lied. Earth will have a source of cheap safe continuous power. The pits will be flooded, the water will absorb all excess radiation. Our atomic power will be harmless to all.'

'Yes?'

'What more do you wish to know?'

'There is a mystery here. I am not satisfied that a mere announcement by the Matriarch can serve to bring peace on Earth. Humans aren't built that way. Fear is too strong within them, the insane logic that forces them to kill so as to keep the race pure. Can you cure that? Can you cure the ingrained instinct of thousands of years?'

'No, but we can change it.' Lyra stared at him with sudden appeal. 'Try and understand, Don. We are doing this for you as well as for us. We are doing this for the race as yet unborn.'

'Doing what?'

'Insanity alters the brain. That has been known for a long time, even before the atomic war men knew that the electrical emissions from an insane mind were not the same as those from a sane one. The electroencephalograph recorded those wave patterns, and they were different.'

'Well?'

'If a man is cruel to the helpless, then he is insane. If he kills his young, he is insane. If anyone does things for the mere sake of wanton destruction, then he is insane.' She paused. 'On that basis, Don, most of the world is at the moment insane.'

'I begin to understand what you mean,' he said, 'but you have not told me everything have you?'

'No. I have told you what is wrong with the world. We can alter that.'

'How?'

She sighed, and glanced again at the instrument on her wrist.

'In the old days when men were insane, one method of treatment was that known as 'shock treatment' or 'electro-therapy'. A current of electricity was passed through the frontal lobes of the brain. Sometimes the results showed an inprovement, at others, there was no discernible change. This was because no man then living knew enough about the nature of the brain, the type of electrical emission, or the wavelength of the radiation necessary to effect a cure. We know more about the brain now than at any time in our history. We can determine the exact wavelength necessary, the exact duration of the shocks, and the inevitable result of such treatment.'

'I see.' Don stared at her with something akin to awe. 'The atomic power! The network of cables to carry the radiation! Shock treatment!'

'Yes. Shock treatment on a worldwide scale. This time tomorrow there will be no insane. No muddled thinking. No hate. No fear. Earth will be whole again, and we, the mutants, will have our chance.'

'But what has the Matriarch to do with all this? Why is she necessary?'

'The last words spoken just before the impact of the radiation will have a special effect. They will affect the subconscious mind, be retained when all else is forgotten. For a space men will sleep, jarred into oblivion by the pulse of radiation. When they awake, the last words to which they have paid concentrated attention will be remembered. I want those words to be aimed at kindness and humanity.'

'I won't do it!' The Matriarch glared at

them from her small eyes. 'It's a trick. I know that it's a trick!'

'No. No, Mary. It's no trick.'

A man stumbled into the room. A thin elderly man with a mane of hair, once white, but now soiled and marred with dirt. His clothes hung in tatters, and his hands were cut, stained with blood and oil. He stared about him with glazed eyes, then smiled as he saw the slumped figure of Le Roy.

'You failed. You tried and you failed.'

'Again?' Le Roy licked his cracked lips. 'But how? I heard you fall, heard you scream. How could you still be alive?'

'You snapped the cable, but did you forget that the platform was held by two? Some debris fell from the stage, and I screamed for good measure.' Moray winced as he stared at his hands.

'I thought that I would never reach the top. The cable cut my fingers to the bone, twice I almost fell into the pit, but I won. I won, Le Roy. Old as I am, I won!'

He turned to the Matriarch.

'Mary, I want you to make that broadcast. For old time's sake if you like, or perhaps because the old can see clearer than the young. We've had our life, perhaps not too good a one, but it was ours to do with as we wished. Give these people their chance.'

'But, John. Will it work as they say?'

'It will work, Mary. Would I have helped them had I thought otherwise? Some will die, the bad cases, the hopelessly insane. Some will die through accident. Others will be stupid, morons, unknowing that they are different from what they were, and uncaring. The vast majority will be sane again. Some for the first time in history. Men will know the kindness of other men, the happiness of true decisions, the wholesome feeling of sheer rightness. We shall feel that too, Mary. You and I, old as we are.'

The video hummed, and the Matriarch looked at the thin pale features of the old doctor. He smiled and threw the switch.

'The world-wide network has been established. Matriarch. Will you speak now?'

'Yes.'

'One moment, Madam. Wait for the red signal.'

The screen swirled, then steadied. Abruptly it flushed a vivid scarlet. The colour faded, returned, faded again, then dyed the screen for a third time. The universal attention signal. All over the world people would watching and listening to the video. Skilled translators would send the words in a thousand different tongues and dialects winging through the air.

Slowly the Matriarch began to speak.

'Peoples of the world hear me. Tonight I have a statement to make unparalleled in the history of the human race. Tonight we stand at the crossing of our future, either we forge ahead into the golden promise of a new and better civilization, or we sink back into the mire of decadence and intellectual death . . .'

Her voice, a voice trained to express just the right degree of emotion, just the exact combination of cliché and metaphor, rose and fell as she put into cunning words the hope of a world. Don squeezed Lyra by the arm.

241

'When will it happen?' he whispered.

'When she has finished. I have the activating control here on my wrist. When I press the stud, the signal will release the radio fuses, and flood the network with the accumulated radiation.'

She smiled up into his intent young face.

'Are you afraid?'

'No. Not now. Not with you beside me.' He smiled at her, and she blushed in sudden understanding.

' . . . and so this old world will rise again. Rise like a Phoenix from the ashes of its dead self, a new and better world.'

She paused, head thrown proudly back as she stared at the screen.

Lyra pressed the stud on her wrist.

A pale wash of blue twinkled on the horizon. A glimmering tide of radiant energy, healing, calming, purifying diseased minds and cleansing unhealthy thoughts. It flashed, spread, and Don held tight to the secretary's slender hand.

With her fingers twined in his, they stood waiting the rebirth of a world.